THE ESCAPE PLAN

The Inception

KRISHANG AGRAWAL

Ukiyoto Publishing

All global publishing rights are held by

Ukiyoto Publishing

Published in 2023

Content Copyright © Krishang Agrawal

ISBN 9789360164812

All rights reserved.
No part of this publication may be reproduced,
transmitted, or stored in a retrieval system, in any
form by any means, electronic, mechanical,
photocopying, recording or otherwise, without the
prior permission of the publisher.

The moral rights of the author have been asserted.

This is a work of fiction. Names, characters, businesses,
places, events, locales, and incidents are either the
products of the author's imagination or used in a
fictitious manner. Any resemblance to actual persons,
living or dead, or actual events is purely coincidental.

This book is sold subject to the condition that it shall
not by way of trade or otherwise, be lent, resold, hired
out or otherwise circulated, without the publisher's
prior consent, in any form of binding or cover other
than that in which it is published.

www.ukiyoto.com

*To Dadu
and my family
Forever and Always*

Acknowledgement

The Escape Plan is my first work. I initially started writing it when I was thirteen and continued to do so until the age of seventeen. I went through most of the things that novice authors typically confront throughout these years. I experienced my first long writer's block at fourteen and didn't write anything until I was fifteen, but I never stopped thinking about it. Later, during the pandemic, I was resting on my couch when I encountered an idea to proceed forward. That one idea brought life to this story. One specialty of this novel is that as I grow up, the main character's maturity level throughout the story also increases.

All of this is only possible because of my loved ones, who have always motivated me to write this work of art and showcase my creativity.

A beloved blessing from my Grandpa, Late Rameshchandra Agrawal, for being the most lovable and cheerful Dadu to ever exist. You're remembered in my heart and soul for eternity to come.

A huge thanks to my Parents, Chetan Agrawal and Smita Agrawal, who were with me at every step and provided me with critics that helped me better find loopholes and errors. I consider myself lucky to be surrounded by this constellation of brilliant and generous people who have helped me grow into who I am today. They proofread my work constantly to find errors and fix them.

I would like to thank my Grandma, Chanda Agrawal, and Uncle, Shekhar Agrawal, for blessing me with success all my life and motivating me when needed. Also, I am thankful to my aunt Monika Agrawal, who gave me comments and steps to improve my work early on.

I couldn't ask for stronger people to make this novel possible.

I'd like to thank my brother, Raghav Agrawal, and my cousins Manasvi Lath, Riya Gupta, and Aarav Lath, who read and critiqued my book early on.

Shivika Jain, my friend and peer, reviewed and read my book to offer me some opinions and motivated me to write and publish this book. Additionally, a big thanks to all my friends involved in motivating me and being there when I needed them the most.

A huge, generous thanks to Ukiyoto Publishers for spotting the potential in the book I always believed it had and helping me throughout the process.

You, people, were really the hidden building blocks for this novel.

Contents

Chapter 1	1
Chapter 2	3
Chapter 3	31
Chapter 4	41
Chapter 5	50
Chapter 6	61
Chapter 7	71
Chapter 8	96
Chapter 9	112
Chapter 10	118
Chapter 11	132
Chapter 12	151
About the Author	*190*

Chapter 1

Two men just passed by contrary to the barrier. I can feel the shadows of another pair go now. They sounded in a hurry. The two guards on both ends of the barrier buzzed monotonously. I want to know what is going on, but I can barely see through by dint of a highly translucent barrier.

The spectral-tinted room is undoubtedly significant. I can barely walk to discover every bit of it. Blood is dripping down my eyelashes, sometimes running into the eye. I am lying on the bed, which is quite comfy but is now stained purple. I struggle to get up from the bed. I push myself up. I walk limping to the stupid creepy camera to look straight into its lens. The limp is getting better, but I think there's something with a muscle up the thigh. I stared at it for five straight minutes. I felt silly and limped back down to the bed. I dropped myself to the floor, my knees hugging my chest and face down. I am feeling sorry. Sorry for whatever I did. All the choices that led me here. Every single step I took made me feel sorry now. I break down. I cannot handle this, but I have to! I am not ready to fight this off. I don't want to be a part of this shit. I don't want to know who I am. I am not ready to be who I am. *But I have to.*

THE PAST

Chapter 2

Crack! Something's broken. It's me. My dad came to me running, reading today's headlines from The Daily Paper, while mom shouted from the other side of the house doing laundry, "What Happened, Aaron?"

Well, that was not as I expected. I have shattered another plate this week. She stood at the kitchen step staring at me for a colossal silly felony, while dad scoffed away sipping off tea from his black matted everyday mug.

Yes, I believe it's normal as I began doing the dishes just two weeks ago, though I admit shattering the fourth plate this morning. Wait... no fifth plate!

Mistakes do happen, right?

I closed the tap. Dad sighed and went away. Mom groaned as she started cleaning and picking up the broken pieces of the plate.

"Go, now! I'll wash the leftover utensils. Go get yourself another work for today."

I moved out of the mess, crossing a dripping ceiling moistening the wooden floor. Why ain't anyone paying attention to this? I hastily arranged a bucket down the roof. And that loud discomfort sound of the first few droplets of water striking the surface of the bucket hurts. I went to my room and closed the door. That hurting sound eased. I unlocked the window as I rolled up the curtains.

It was a dull, boring cloudy day in December. The clock was striking eight in the morning. The winds were soothing, and the pain just faded away. A cool breeze was flowing through the air. There was fog thickening the neighborhood with no sightings of the Sun. Thick enough that I could barely see the local dogs running by, jostling and barking in the wind. A cold breeze just drove around me, and I shivered.

"What a day," I sighed.

"Aaron! Can you sweep the house? I could see dust all around?" Dad's voice encountered from another room. "Be quick."

"Our house is already a mess, Dad," I mumbled. "On it!" I shouted. I took the sweeper from the storeroom and began sweeping the floor.

My house was a mess. Old *crackling* wood floor stained with tea-color-whitened walls and doors all scratched, but we finally had a dining table and a second-handed sofa with springs coming over. This cracked house was twenty-third to the Reticent Route.

I belong to a financially low middle-class family, always wearing that red T-shirt and worn-out black pants with a daily casual haircut. A pointed nose with a dimple on the left cheek. Shoes with a pair of socks.

Due to the distinct situations and living at the city's border, I was unaware of the world and the people around me. I never went to the marketplace of the city, and situations never came as such. I never went to school and never asked my parents to.

My father used to work as a shoe seller, and in which he used to earn only a couple of dollars. Every year on my birthday, he used to bring a pair of shoes for me by collecting one-fourth of the salary he used to earn as a shoe seller. So, I never had a lack of shoes. Though, I have never seen his workplace as I am not allowed to be out for long periods and without any supervision. I wonder how his workplace must be. Given that we do not earn very much, I believe it must be a hall with glass walls at the entrance with a temporary flex at the top and shoes stacked up on numerous shelves along the walls and sitting area- mostly a dull steel bench- on the middle of the wooden carpet, lights at either four corners of the hall. He has gifted me enough shoes that last year I almost cried for a smartphone and went on a rampage after seeing one in the neighborhood. And no, I didn't get it and still longing.

My mother, she's the most multi-talented person I have ever met. But can't fulfill her dreams due to some financial problems. And I learned everything: to write, read, and spell; in other words, I was home-schooled by my mother. She's a Bachelor's in Accountancy. She tried but couldn't catch a break for a job. A couple of days ago, she gave an interview to be an accountant at Hallop Bank.

On that cloudy day, things started to get better for worse. Dad was finished with his work. The clock was at ten when dad sat on a dining chair. I was sitting right next to him. He received an SMS on his cell phone from his manager. I managed to peek into his cell phone. He checked it.

Ethan Jerez,

*You're one of the most skillful employees in our company. May this company touch higher skies and win the best shoe manufacturing industry this year. But for that, we need employees like you. The one who convinces the customer. So, I hope you will be glad to **know** that you have received a reward of four hundred dollars as a bonus for your work.*

Dad and I jumped with joy. "Woohoo!" Exclaimed dad while he was having a tap dance. Mom came running from the laundry, "What's happening? Why is your dad dancing, and why do you two seem so happy?" Asked mom. "Have we won a lottery?"

"No, Jess, I have got a bonus of four hundred dollars!" said dad. He stopped dancing and announced dramatically, "Pack your bags, get ready, and wash yourselves, we're going on a long drive."

"Long drive?" Mom and my face rose. "Okay, just give me half an hour." She said and went off smirking.

"I shall go and get the car from those weirdos." Dad went away. I could hear the main gate close. I think he left.

Those weirdos just came from nowhere. A week ago, they just came here by car. Before their arrival here, an unknown and mysterious object was seen, and tremors were felt across the town. When they arrived in an awful blue-colored car, one of them agitatedly got out of the vehicle licking an ice cream frantically. It was a boy around my age. He looked around like he was scared. He almost crunched the waffle cone into chunks.

"Clear," he said.

Another one got out. It was a woman. She, too, seemed nervous. She moved her shaky hands and made some indications, and pointed to the house like she was giving an order. Someone in the driving seat drove the car to the house's parking lot next to us. It had trouble parking that car. The car moved backward and forward. Finally, the car was parked slant. And the final one got out. It was a man. He, too, appeared worried. *Instead,* they all looked nervous. Their hands were shivering. They just moved into the house following ours.

"Come on," shouted dad from outside while in the car honking the horn. "We gotta get-go!"

"Wait, just five more minutes." She quickly got to the kitchen and filled up a bottle. She saw me passing by the kitchen. "Are you ready, kid?"

"Yeah!" I spoke. "I strapped my watch on my wrist, combed my hair, and wore my favorite T-shirt. And now, I was going to get in the car. You want something?"

"No, just get in the car." She switched off the light in the kitchen. We moved out of the house, and mom closed the gate.

We got into the car, and off we went.

It's been two hours since we left our home. I thought this car looked awful just from the exterior, but now I know it's also horrible from the inside. But, something's better than nothing.

The car had a GPS, the most helpful thing in the car, and, unfortunately, a cassette tape player. (Who has it in cars these days). We drove through farms and fields, and mom bought her favorite cassette tape. She placed it in the player and increased the volume. That song's just annoying. I had explained to mom several times that it's the most disliked music of all time, but she never listened.

Mom and dad got lost in that song. I plugged my ears with my fingers, so my ears didn't bleed. Dad revved up the car. I looked out of the window. I pressed the button to open the window. The glass slid down. The sound was pleasing for a second. I put my head out. I squinched my eyes, and the wind hit hard on my face. The winds were faster than a running horse. Something to bet on. I could see tall and wavy crops dancing around the fields in the December light. It was so relaxing. Some had carrots, and others had Wheatfield. The wheat fielders just stopped sowing seeds and looked continuously at our car. It's the only car running on this highway. Some climbed down the tractors; others dropped all their equipment and sprinted towards the car. They felt like they were having trouble running.

They raged, "Stop, you must be him." They cried.

There were dozens of them running behind the car. Mom and dad were still beguiled by the songs. I tried to tell them, but they were not responding and shrugged me off to enjoy the music. I was terrified. I looked back at them. Some people came running from nowhere and caught them behind. I looked around. The carrot fields were empty. It was creepy. Was I hallucinating? I need something to eat.

It was afternoon. We still haven't had lunch. We were still starving. Having not eaten anything was driving us crazy. There were no restaurants nearby. "Food," I mourned. Dad turned on the GPS to see the nearest restaurant. The nearest restaurant was about thirty miles away, and it shows a forty-five-minute route to the restaurant. "Food." I mourned again.

"Just hold on a bit more, son," Mom said. Dad accelerated the car. It thundered and revved louder.

The car reached a mark of a hundred kilometers per hour. I could see birds behaving oddly. The fields were far gone, and we were now on the forest highway. I could feel myself approaching the restaurant. Within the next ten minutes, we reached the point. The restaurant was just at the entrance of the woods. We arrived thirty minutes early than what the GPS had estimated. I got out and stretched myself. We got into the lunchroom.

"Welcome to Diners Vila," a woman welcomed us. "We have been waiting for so long."

"What? What do you mean by 'you are waiting for so long?" Dad stammered.

"No. Only a few know about this route. Only any people go through this *wane* highway." She clarified and grinned.

"I think we should not be here. They occur precisely to those weirdos, don't you, Jessie?" Dad mumbled to mom so quietly that almost anyone beyond a one-meter radius won't hear.

"Yeah, they do. But we have no alternate choice. The next restaurant is another fifty miles ahead." mom said, looking at me. "We have to."

Dad gave me a dejected look and booked us a table near the windows. The woman guided us to table twenty-four, clothed with a blue blanket with mysterious lines near a giant circular window.

There was no one there except us. All the tables were vacant, but it seems someone already had a great meal almost a while ago. The same woman came to us and handed over the menu. I took the menu. The menu was made of different materials I had never touched or seen. I opened it. The menu lists bizarre food items.

- Terrain soup
- Annelids pepperoni salted flat pie
- A hound Burger
- Sapien salad
- Schhafiu specie roasted legs

"What the...?" I threw up a bit in my mouth. I flipped the card and read the menu card's cover. The menu card says 'Alien Sustenance.'

"No, son. It's... it's... um...What is written here?" Mom asked her. She gave a glimpse at it. She then quickly snatched it from my hand.

"Sorry for the inconvenience, ma'am," she apologized. My son. He loves to play around with his code language. I'll bring you another." She turned and brisked to the kitchenette.

"How did you? How do you know what's written on it? How did you know his son's code language?" Mom asked me a bunch of questions. The waitress walked with one hand behind her back and the other holding the menu and handed over it to dad. Dad checked it. It was appropriate. No stupid inane scribblings of her son now. She stood formally beside the table.

"So, son, answer me. How do you know?" She asked me with half-closed eyes. Dad was looking for the cheap food items on the menu list.

"I don't know. I just guessed. The phrase just popped up in my mind when I read that. I also didn't decode it because I don't know his son or code language." I explained to her, but she still looked at me with suspicious eyes and then laughed. The woman was possibly hearing me. Her eyes were on me. She was giving me a sharp look.

Dad ordered three tortilla chicken soups and one chicken peri-peri with extra butter. The woman noted it in her notepad. She repeated the order for confirmation. Then she went to her kitchenette. "Aren't you ordering too much and expensive, dear," Mom asked dad.

"Come on, Jessie! I have got a bonus, and I am just giving you and Aaron a treat." Dad said. "Don't worry, we have a lot of money right now. Just enjoy."

Within the next few minutes, the lunch was on the table. Butter was flowing down the gleaming brown flawless chicken. The soup seems delightful. "Sporty serving!" Dad exclaimed. The woman served us water and stood formally beside the table.

"I will have the leg piece," I announced, lifting my right hand.

We chuckled and had lunch. My stomach was complete to my neck. She was still there standing and watching us (specifically me!). I left some of my soup and told her to pack it up for me. She took my soup and went away to the kitchenette.

"What a luscious lunch, isn't it, dad?

"Yeah, had this sort of lunch years ago, isn't it, Jessie?" Dad asked mom lavishly. Dad dabbed his mouth richly with his napkin.

"Oh, Yes. Thank you for bringing us here, Ethan." Mom, too, dabbed her mouth plushly with her napkin.

"I think I should go and wash my hands?" I asked them, rising.

Mom gave me approval. The washroom must be near the kitchenette, as implied on the board. I walked towards it and stood near the door. I looked around for the restroom and walked in. It was pretty technologized. I could also hear distinct voices from the kitchenette.

"Okay, STAGE – 1 is complete." The woman asserted. "We are now looking for STAGE – 2. Get all things ready soon."

I neglected it. As it's their business, and it doesn't make any sense to me, so I focused on my hands. I held my hands under the tap in front of a red sensor. A red ray scanned my hands and said in a computerized voice, "Specie not found. Water." The water instantly splashed onto my hands. I washed my hands. The water flowed for the next ten seconds.

Dad called up for the bill. She came with the soup in a cylindrical container wrapped up in brown foil and with the bill card. She gave the bill card to dad and the soup to me. Dad opened it. "Where's the bill receipt?" asked dad to her.

"Don't worry, sir, you are our first customer today. So, we decided to give you an advantage. We give *'food in your budget'* offer to our every first customer." She said. "Didn't you read our flyer?"

"Oh! So that's the thing!" Dad exclaimed with gleaming eyes. Dad took out his wallet and kept ten dollars in it. "Thank you."

"Thank you, sir." She said and went to the kitchenette. We stood up, and mom pulled out all the napkins from the napkin holder and kept them in her purse.

We then walked to the car and got in. And continued our journey. We entered the forest highway full of old full-grown dried oak trees scattering the light through them to the soft bed of crunchy dried leaves unwinding on the spiked green grass of the woods.

We escaped through the woods and drove through various farms and fields. Mom also plucked apples and stole full-grown wheat from the eyes of their owners. She kept it in the car's trunk.

It was evening. On the way home, we passed through the farm lane crossing numerous fields. We passed the woods. "Mom, where did it go?!" I asked her with my eyes and pointed out to a rectangular vast barren area. My hands were shivering with fear.

"Now what, son?" Mom and dad looked out of the window, half-afraid. They saw what I saw. A whole rectangular arid region bordered with field crops. Dad shivered as he searched ballistically for the flashlight. He pulled open the glove compartment and blindly looked for the flashlight. He was gasping as he took the flashlight out and torched through the window.

The field was burned triangularly to ashes and crops around were either burned or broken. Fear flowed down our eyes.

"Where… where did it go? We had our lunch here about six hours ago. Where in the world could it possibly go?!" Mom expressed frightenedly. "It's… it's impossible!"

"They're here, Jess," Dad muffed into the air and stared frightened at mom. "They know."

Mom's eyes turned back to dad as they locked eyes and she appeared to muster up some courage after she nodded to what dad said.

"Who are here?" I exclaimed. "What are you two talking about? We need to get away now. This appears to be some sought of black sorcery."

Dad flicked off the flashlight and tossed it back in the glove box. She took a deep breath and looked straight at the road.

"I think we all are exhausted and fatigued. That's why we are all talking claptrap. Let's just drive home." Dad said. "We all need rest."

He revved the car and moved away from the plot. On the way, all the carrot and wheat fields were empty. (That might be because it's dusk already.)

We bought pizza for dinner while we were on the way home. After a few minutes, we were on the lane home. I peeked into the GPS to see the time. It was twenty-six past eight. We were home before half-past eight.

Dad parked the car in front of our house. Dad unlocked the car's trunk and mom took out all the stolen supplies (Fruit and wheat). I got out of the car and looked at my house.

"Home sweet home," I sighed.

Mom asked me to get off all our luggage from the car and even take all the chocolate wrappers and chips waste. I did as it is my mother asked me to do.

Dad drove the car to the house next to us. Dad honked the horn and called for the male weirdo.

"Hey, Evian! Come get your car. We are home." His son came up. His red smudgy cheeks, messy hair, and fatty baby hands still held ice cream. Doesn't he catch a cold in this December winter munching on just ice creams?

"Hey, not you Cosmo," dad smirked. "Where's your dad? Call him." Dad said, smiling.

"He's out. Come later. Bye." He said impassively. He turned and was about to get into his house when he galloped the whole waffle cone into his explanatory big mouth.

"Hey, wait!" dad exclaimed. He stopped facing his back. "I am parking it here. Tell your dad when he comes."

He walked and got into the house. "What a jerk, man!" Dad exclaimed. "Aaron, help me park the car."

I helped him with directions to park the car carefully and called Cosmo.

This time it took a while for him to come. He slammed the door and looked at us irritably. "Here, the keys!" Dad exclaimed. "Sorry to disturb you, Cosmo."

Another ice cream cone crowned his hand. This time he tried what-it-looked strawberry than his regular vanilla. Neat!

He walked down, snatched the keys from him, and walked away madly into the house. "Blockhead," Dad mumbled.

Mom had already gotten into the house, and dad took the excess luggage kept in front of our home.

Dad and I moved into the house, and I closed the door behind us. The Sun shifted below the horizon. The clock was striking nine. Mom called us into the dining for dinner.

I had a cheese pizza with extra olives and capsicum. Mom and dad had pepperoni pizza with extra cheese. We starving beings ate a whole regular-sized pizza and went off to sleep. There were muffled noises of loud arguments that night from another corner of the house.

We were having breakfast. Dad was reading the newspaper and was having food. I looked at the back of the newspaper. It was the front page. Dad had a weird habit of reading the newspaper from the back. He did so because dad always wanted to read the main headlines at the end.

The first headline says:

ANOTHER MURDER BY *THE ASSASSIN BREAKERS! Dated 12th of December*

I still regret on my bad habit that I don't read the whole content. The doorbell rang. My father said to open the door, so I got up from the dining table and stepped out of the room. I reached for the door and opened it. The letter was dropped in our Mailbox. A note was written on it. It said:

TO JESSICA JEREZ

23, JEREZ'S SHACK, RETICENT ROUTE.

I hurried towards the dining room and entered the kitchen. I handed over the letter to my mother. She broke the seal and flipped out the letter, and read:

· · · · ·

Well, Jessica, we are here to tell you that you have been selected for a job in our bank. You will be paid well, and if you want to accept our offer, you have to call within ten days of receiving the letter. We will let you know the other information on the phone. Phone no. 473574****

Senior Manager,

Hallop Bank

· · · · ·

She was in a whirl of joy. Dad and mom danced with joy. But I was not so happy after hearing that news.

"What a load of luck!" Cried, Mom.

"Yesterday, you got the bonus for your work, and today I got work," she told dad.

Then without any word, she took her phone and dialed the number.

"Hello." A deep voice encountered her ear.

"Yeah, um… is this Hallop Bank? I am Jessica Jerez. A letter was dropped on my doorstep this morning saying that I was selected for a job at Hallop Bank. It says to call this number to get more information."

"Yes. This is Hallop Bank, and um… let me check your name J…E…S….S….I….C…A… and here it is, yeah you have been selected as an assistant accountant in our bank. Come to our Hallop bank within 5 days after this call if you want to join the job. A final interview will be taken there."

"Strange but why not? I'll be there. Thank you."

"You're most welcome. Best of luck!"

She hung up the phone and danced with joy. At that moment, without any question or anything, she took her step towards her bedroom, took a suitcase, opened her cupboard, and searched and filled the clothes in the bag.

My father and I were looking at each other with a lot of curiosity and questions. Then within an hour, she was done packing up her clothes and requirements, which she had never used for years. She was not looking as before, but my father and I were still looking at each other curiously. I stood on my dining chair, and we went to her. She looked as if she was about to leave.

She pushed my dad back and moved to the house's main gate with the same luggage she used for the trip with a bit of customization by adding her clothes to it.

My father took her hand with drops of water in his eyes and said, "It would be good if you stayed with us only for this night. Can you? Please."

She looked toward him and locked eyes.

"I'm sorry I rushed through it without consulting anyone, especially you, Ethan."

"It's okay. It happens," he said. "You must also be fatigued by tomorrow's trip, right?"

"Yeah, I am." She said and dad pulled her up while she was fainting.

When I saw them hugging, I too gave them a hug. After exchanging hugs for a while, we all went to the dining room to eat breakfast. She wasn't feeling well, so Dad brought her to the bedroom. It was a successful afternoon and evening. I recall my father securing his cash in a cabinet. I was constantly bothered by those weirdos ranting, as was probably the entire neighborhood.

Then things started to get worse with no hope of getting better, which finally happened.

We went to the dining room and sat on our dining chairs at night. I served the chicken soup in the bowl to all members. Mom poured and filled the glasses of water for the members. After this afternoon, she was feeling better as she took some pills and medicine as prescribed by our neighborhood house doctor.

Dad served the salads on each plate. We prayed and started eating dinner. I finished the first, kept my plate in the sink, and washed my hands. I walked beyond the dining room through the door and went to my bedroom to sleep, as it was already eleven. I was also tired due to the events that happened throughout the day. I laid down on the bed, blanketed myself, and closed my eyes, then within half an hour, I was asleep.

At about two or three in the darkness of night, my sleep broke, and I was awake in bed thirsty. I stood up and walked out through my bedroom door and headed toward the kitchen. I entered the kitchen, picked up the bottle, flipped the cap, and as I brought it towards my mouth, I heard a noise. I stopped, flipped back the lid, and kept the bottle on the dining table. I again listened to the same voice. I was freaked out, but I built up the courage and walked toward the voice. I followed the voice. The faster I walk, the louder it gets. In the blackness of night, I was walking and following the voice, I felt a tangible thing in front of me. I was freaked out. My heart was pounding and almost skipped a beat. I inspected the thing. I was relaxed when I came to know that it was the door. I opened the door a little without making any noise and listened. It was my mom and dad. They were shouting at each other over some topic. And I heard a thing which I should not.

"Oh my god, they're here," said mom. "Why do you appear so relaxed, shithead?"

"You are always so tensed, dear. They won't hurt us."

"How are you so sure? We have what they want!"

"We do, and that is why they won't hurt us." He said coming closer to her and holding her in his arms. His arms were around her waist.

She hugged him.

"What if he comes to know he's not one of us? He's just a teen."

"You remember where we found him?"

"Yeah. In a desert, abandoned by his own. Set alone to survive and fight this world."

He chuckled and she hugged him tighter.

"I wonder sometimes what if he comes to know?"

"Know what?

"He's not ours," she said. "That we adopted him."

"He won't, I swear."

"Really?"

"I have an idea-"

I was shocked. I was choking on my tears. It felt like a lump in my throat and tears blinked down. My ears tried to puff the information back out. My brain running. I held myself to the wall, closed the door quietly, and walked towards my door wretched.

I reached my room and closed the door behind me. I cannot forget or overthrow that thought from my mind. I sat on the bed, crying. Slowly I leaned on the ground feeling lonely and helpless. A bucketful of tears tore down my eyes to face and then to the old wooden floor. I cried at least for three to four hours, pouring the room's wooden floor into a lake of tears in which ants and small insects could easily swim. My tear-stained face was puffy and swollen with grief. Hours passed as I stayed gutted onto the ground. It was seven in the morning. My so-called mother was about to leave. My father called me up to say goodbye to her.

I stood up from the floor, swiped up the tears from my swollen eyes, washed my face, opened the door, and stepped out of the room. I saw the house. It was not looking as it did before. Nothing seems to be mine now - the gate, the walls, the photos, and everything else.

I turned and looked towards the door. The main entrance was opened, the clouds were gone, and the sky was evident as the crystal-clear lake. A beam of yellowish-orange eye-hurting rays of sunlight hit the laminated glass side of the photo frame lying on the floor and reflected into my eyes. I could not open my eyes, and as I was trying to open them, it was willing to close. I stepped and walked towards the main door half-blind. I stretched my hand and reached for the knob of the door.

I opened the gate wide so that it could fit my body.

I stepped and passed through the main door. I literally can see only white in this marvelous light. I felt a little pain in opening up my eyes. I continuously blinked my eyes for four to five seconds to see everything clearly. As my eyes were clear. I saw that Mom was leaving and Dad was calling me to say goodbye.

I walked down the doorstep and unwillingly hugged her and said goodbye to her.

Mom, too, said goodbye.

The tears in her eyes, she turned backward and walked and walked and gone. Dad was still standing there until her shadow went off. He was crying (not literally crying, but the drops of tears were in his eyes). Then suddenly, Dad put his hand over my shoulder.

"Are you gonna miss her?"

"Probably not," I answered.

He looked at me and gave me a heartful smile like I was joking, but he didn't know I wasn't. Dad walked into the house through the door. I stood out, turning back to get into the house. The weirdos were still watching over me from behind the windows. All three seemed happy after my mom left. As they noticed me watching them, they quickly covered the windows. I moved into my house before I would go mad over them. I closed the door. Dad was still standing there and asked when he saw me.

"Want to have breakfast?"

"Yeah, I would love to, but before that. I want to ask you how that photo frame fell there?"

"Oh, that. I am sorry I ignored it. That may be because of the cat."

"Cat?" I asked with surprise.

"Yes, our neighborhood cat, which comes into one of our society's houses every night."

"Then, why didn't you ever tell me?"

"You never asked."

"Okay…"

"Now, come inside and have your breakfast."

I picked up the frame facing the wooden side. I turned it over to see the photo. It was the family photo taken two or three years back at my uncle's wedding. I kept the photo frame back on the cabinet.

I went into the kitchen, sat on the dining table, and took some leftover old stale bread. I put some red color jam on it and ate it. While eating, I thought maybe my dream was broken because that cat made the frame fall and broke my sleep. After breakfast, I washed my hands and walked to my bedroom. Dad cleaned the shattered pieces of the broken glass frame.

I entered and closed the door behind me. I sat on my bed, closed my eyes, and started thinking about last night's episode.

Was it a dream? Am I not their child? Was all I heard true? If they are not my parents, then who are my real parents? I had a lot of questions in mind.

I put more pressure on my brain. 'Am I really from this city? Then from where do I belong? Am I ever gonna..?' I knocked delivered on my door. I was interrupted.

I drove my fingers through my hair. I opened my eyes. My head was in a whirl. Another knock on the door was delivered. I was still in a whirl. Another knock was delivered by a voice. "Is everything okay? Can I come in?"

After two to three minutes, I was back to normal. With my head down, I answered, "Come in."

The door cracked and swung open. I looked up and saw my dad in a funky outfit. "Are you going somewhere?" I asked him.

"Yes," he replied.

I got a call on the landline from the boss of the shoe shop. He said that all the workers had been called up urgently for something, and you should tell all workers by calling them on their landlines and phones. He then hung up the phone. I then called every worker I knew whose landline numbers I had written up in my phone book.

"Okay," I said. "So, when are you going to come?"

"I'll be back before midnight as we all workers had planned to have our dinner outside, so…, you know."

"So then what about me?"

"You can have your yesterday's leftover tortilla soup, and for dinner, you can cut and have some vegetables or fruits."

I nodded my head slightly. He handed me the keys to the house and doors. I slid it into my pocket. "Goodbye then." He patted his hand on my shoulder and smiled. I also smiled at him feeling awkward. He then walked near the door and soon walked out, closing the room from behind. I was losing my mind, and I knew it. I heard the main door close.

I laid back on my bed and closed my eyes. I thought of every moment that happened last night.

Waking up in my bed

Entering the kitchen

Flipping the bottle's cap

Hearing and then following the voice

Opening the door, and

Hearing *I am not their child.*

I was getting depressed as time passes, weeping inconsolably biting onto the pillow, trying to hide in it, tangled up in the bedsheet. My eyes swoll heavily, and I could not keep them open long enough then. As a result, I passed out.

It was afternoon.

I was still in bed sleeping. Then, suddenly I woke up. My eyes were wide open. I stood up from my bed instantly and looked at my wall clock. It was half-past one. A headache knocked on my fractured disposition. I quickly walked out of the room and walked to the kitchen looking out for tortilla soup. While searching, I found a cat supping my tortilla soup. Hot under the collar, I ran over to drive the cat away. The cat jumped through the window and ran out. I glanced at my tortilla soup. It was all spoiled. Its hair floats into it. Unfortunately, I picked it up and threw it in the dustbin beside the sink. That afternoon I had to starve for food. Then again, I went to my room, closed it, and put my head under the pillow. All these things that happened last night were coming continuously into my thoughts. I tried not to, but these thoughts were killing me. This time the ideas were getting over my head, and it seemed that these thoughts were brainwashing me.

At last, after so and so much thinking and killing thoughts. I came to a result. ***I decided to leave my house.***

I know that this sounds overly dramatic, but I would rather not choose to live with them and never tell them what happened last night but leave the house and start a new journey. I cannot live my whole life with them hiding this, and even starting a new journey sounds fun!

Chapter 3

I stood up from the bed, pulled up my bedroom drawer, and searched for my bag pack. After searching for fifteen minutes, I found it in my parents' suitcase. I grabbed one of the bag's straps and pulled it out. I closed the bed drawer and threw my bag on the bed.

I opened my cupboard and searched for clothes. I kept three T-shirts, two shirts and a pair of shoes. I took some accessories like a comb and a tube of body lotion.

I knew I had forgotten something but didn't know whether to take it. Yes, I was talking about money because nothing could happen without it. I had keys. I slid my fingers inside my pocket, looked for the keys, and took them out. A bad feeling crept into my body, but I had to do it. Like a thief, I walked out of my room and quietly toward my parents' room. I reached the door, looked at the key in my hand, and searched for the doorknob. I found the doorknob and inserted the key in the doorknob. I twisted the key, and a cracked, loud voice encountered my ear in the noise of silence. Leaving the key inserted, I opened the door and stepped inside the room. And another tragedy happened. I entered the room and closed the door, not knowing that the key was still in the door knob. I was walking on my toes, and every time I stepped, a crack noise encountered from the wooden floor, which was usual in my house every time we walked, but now, this time, it felt like I would be caught by this slight noise (now hearing like dinosaur roar).

I reached the cupboard and looked at the door key. Whenever my parents went outside the house, I knew they kept their cupboard key under their pillow covers. I climbed on the bed and took the first pillow. I put my hand inside the pillow cover and searched for the key. It was not in the first one. I took the second one and did the same. Then the streak of failures continued.

"Not In the second one," I said. I looked in third, fourth, and fifth, but I need help.

The last one was left. I took God's name (who's probably not supporting me) and picked up the last one. Positively I said, "It's always the last one." With this optimism, I put my hand inside the pillow cover. I searched for it on the first side and found nothing. Then I pulled my hand out and put my hand on another side. I searched for it again. "Found it!"

I held the key with my fingers and pulled my hand out. I had the keys between my two fingers. I put the key on my left palm. There were five keys in the ring. I separated the pillow from the others. I walked down the bed and inserted one of the keys into the door lock. The cracking noise of unlocking the cupboard occurred. "Lucky me!"

I opened the cupboard, pulled up a drawer, and took a hundred dollars out of three hundred dollars from a small container box. I kept the money in my pocket, feeling like a professional thief. I kept the box back in its original place. I closed the drawer and the cupboard by twisting the key to the left. I returned the key from the doorknob and put it into my pocket. I adjusted and put back all the pillows as it was before. I felt so much guilt for stealing money from my dad's bonus he earned by working there for years. But I had no other choice.

I walked and went to the door to open it. When I tried to open the door, it won't. I tried again, but it stuck. I pulled it out. I thought there had been some mechanical issue, or it could just be a jam, so I had another try—another big fail. Just then, the thought struck and stuck in my mind. I became so panicked. My heart pounded louder and faster. "How can I just make an incredible mistake?" I mumbled. I slapped and hit myself so severely that my cheeks turned partially red, thinking that how in this world did I not pay attention to it that key's been inserted in the door of this room and, even if I did not pay attention to it but how can I close the door even by mistake (well, it is completed by mistake!) Thinking that, I slapped myself again. That left a mark on it.

The Escape Plan

I sat on the bed and thought of a way to get out of here. I got up and looked at every corner of the room to get out, but none was except one—the windows. I walked towards the windows and tried to open them. It won't. I tried again—another failure. Then a sudden thought stuck in my mind that it would be locked. I stretched out my hand and reached for the keys in my pocket. I took the keys and inserted one of them into the window lock. It did not open. Then I tried another one. It won't. I tried third. None of that rings the bell. I finally tried the last one, inserted the key, and rotated it.

"Crack!"

This key was it. I left the key inserted in the window lock. I pushed the windows. It swung open. I jumped through the window, and you know what? I was out of my house. I ran and went to the kitchen window. The window was unlocked. I looked around.

Cosmo watched me from the other side of their window, licking a vanilla softy.

"Shit!" I exclaimed, trying to act normal.

I acted like I was watering the plants, although I was not.

"He couldn't see through the walls." I gasped and smirked. "Hi," I shouted. He walked away, licking it.

"Thank God, he's gone!" I sighed. I quickly climbed the window. I kept one of my legs on the sink and then another. I jumped, and I was in the house.

I was much more relaxed now. It was like pulling out a tooth from a dragon's mouth. I walked and went to their door. I reached there and saw that the key had been inserted. I rotated the key to open the door. The door was opened. I pushed the door, and it swung open. Now, with no other mistake, I entered the room. I reached for the window and pulled it back to close it. The window was together, and I returned the key to complete it. The cracking noise indicated that the window had been closed. I pulled back the key and searched for the pillow where I found the key. I found and took the pillow, which I kept separate from the others.

I took the key and put it back into the pillow cover. I rearranged all the pillows and kept them in their original places. I corrected every tiny detail in the room – the pillows, the bed cover, and every other attribute to avoid getting caught. I slowly stepped out of the room without changing or disturbing any room detail. I stepped out of the room through the door, which was opened, and locked it back. I pulled out the key and kept it back in my pocket. I closed my eyes, feeling relaxed, and thought, "It was like plucking a tooth from Lion's mouth."

I opened my eyes and realized I was full of sweat, and its drops were falling to the ground. I walked to the bathroom and swung the door open. I entered and pushed on the light. I opened the tap of the washbasin. The water was chilly. I poured water into my hands and gave a splash on my face. A tremendous feeling runs through my body. I then wiped up my face with a towel hanging beside the washbasin. I was feeling much better now. I stepped out of the bathroom and closed the door from behind. I then turned off the light in the bathroom. I leaned towards the wall and turned my head towards the wall clock. It was three in the afternoon. And now, I had to decide when I had to leave the house.

I straightened myself and thought for a while. After giving an elephant load, I decided to leave the house after twelve hours, precisely at three o'clock in the morning or three hours after midnight. I walked to my room, fixing this final decision in my mind. I entered and closed the door from behind. I checked my pockets. There were keys in one of the pockets, and in the other, there was money. I pulled out the money from my pocket and counted it. It licked my thumb and started calculating it. It was perfect—the perfect 100 dollars. I kept the money back in my pocket. I was tired, and my eyes were heavy, like lifting a bucket full of water. They were telling me to give them a little relaxation.

I decided to relax for a while. I laid my body on my bed and closed my eyes. As I closed my eyes, I felt a relaxation flow in my body. And soon, I was asleep.

I had flashes. I was floating up in the sky... It's all really bright! I cannot feel my... body! I am... on a bed? A metallic one... My body aches everywhere. I dozed off! Wait, what now? My stomach is wide-open, and I am awake! I can't feel anything, though. It's all blurry. It's scary! I want to Scream! Am I screaming? Mostly not; I can't hear myself... I see some figures. Who are they? HELP! HELP! I scream. I can't hear. Am I doing it all in the brain? I hear a faint voice.

"Implant the translator... His brain... neck... the memories."

I dozed off.

I woke up abruptly. Was it a dream? It must be. My heart's pounding maniacally. It was such an awful dream, primarily due to distress. I raised myself to sit on the bed. I was feeling recharged. Better than ever! I recalled whatever happened. I could not see around correctly. Rubbing my eyes, I turned my head upwards and looked at the wall clock. I then looked down. I stopped chafing my eyes, and all the dancing lines consolidated into one. My heart's doing better now. Stable. I looked upwards at the wall clock. It was half past ten, and I hadn't eaten dinner. I got up from my bed. My entire body cracked up; I cracked my knuckles, stepped outside the room, and closed the door behind me.

My stomach rumbled badly. I was hungry. I walked to the kitchen and tried to remember what my father had said to me to eat. I remembered and took a cucumber and an apple from the polythene bag kept nearby on the dining table. I took a knife and cut the cucumber into several pieces and an apple into two halves. I placed the slices of cucumber and the two halves of apple onto a plate. I left the kitchen, went to the living hall, and sat on the old, noisy, broken sofa with springs coming over. I ate the cucumber and then the apple. In the next ten to fifteen minutes, my dinner was over. I stood up from the shrieking sofa, which was quite old.

I left the living room, went to the kitchen, and kept my plate in the sink. I washed my hands. When I was about to leave the kitchen, I remembered I had to wash the dish as it was Thursday. Every Friday and Thursday, it was my duty to wash the plates. I turned back and searched for the soap. While searching, I saw the marks of my footprints near the sink. This could have happened when I was entering the house through this window. I thanked God for saving me on this front. I couldn't have imagined what would have happened if he had seen those tracks. I opened the sink's tap and started cleaning the marks of footprints using my hand. I rubbed my hands repeatedly on the marks to rub and vanish them. Soon the prints vanished. I then washed and cleaned my plate. After washing my plate, I kept it beside the sink.

"Shit!" I exclaimed. A sudden thought struck my mind. "He was gone out, and what if he had come while I was asleep and is in one of the house's rooms?" I washed my hands quickly.

I stepped out of the kitchen and looked and searched in every room for my father. I felt relieved when I knew that he was not home yet. But soon be there. It was quarter past eleven. There was still time left for me to leave the house. I was getting bored and did not have anything to do, so I walked and went to my room to check if everything I packed was proper or have to put something else. I entered and closed the door behind me. I sat on my bed and pulled out my bag pack, which I had to carry with my journey. I brought and placed the bag in the middle of my legs. I ran the chain of the bag to open it. The bag was open. To check everything correctly, I counted and put everything outside the bag: The comb, cream, eatables, clothes, dictionaries (to find the meaning of words if someone used new words in the central-main city), undergarments, a pen, and the most crucial thing in my pocket - the money. I put both hands in my pockets to check whether I had kept the money.

It was not there. I was freaked out. I stood up from my bed and started searching each pocket for money. Nada. I was losing my mind. I looked beneath the bed, beside the bed, or in another phase. I looked at every corner of the room except the top of my bed. I now walked to my bed, catching the last level to bomb up my head with RDX, which I do not have, but I will. I looked at my bed and began searching for the money after searching the bed three to five times. I found the money where I was sitting and counting up my stuff. I was furious at myself, outraged. I grabbed and put the money back into my pocket, thinking and forgiving myself, saying, "At least I found the money."

I then sat back on my bed and arranged and packed everything on the ground into the bag pack. I zipped the chain of the bag and kept it near the bed. I stood up from the bed, stepped out of the room, and closed the door. I looked out at the house. I had nothing to do. I traveled erratically in the whole house. I was bored. Nothing to do at all. I reclined on the floor near the entrance, thinking about what to do.

Chapter 4

The doorbell rang. I was slouched on the floor. My consciousness rose. I cruised up from the floor and straightened myself. Another bell enveloped the house.

"It's probably Dad," I thought.

I gathered myself, fitted clothes, and presided towards the door to open it. I reached for the doorknob and unlocked it. The door swung open with a slight screech. I looked down at the shoes.

The shoes were muddy. I slowly angled my head up, looking at the trousers and the shirt. He was wearing shady grey cotton trousers and an everyday check-patterned shirt. But as far as I can recall, he was wearing his work uniform in the morning that his manager had given him when he started to work there. Thinking about all that, I looked upwards and looked at the face. He was not my dad but an oversized man.

I instantly pulled the door to close it, but the person put on his toe and thwarted the door from closing. I applied more force, but the man was exerting a double solidity. He instantly searched his pocket with one hand and another hand indeed on the door. He pulled his hand out from his pocket and held something in his hand. I quickly looked about to do something. My eyes plunged upon a small three-drawer cabinet arranged near the wall. I stretched out one of my legs and hands to open the drawer. I opened the drawer and grabbed the hammer. I pulled my hand back with the hammer, grasped it tightly, and lashed it as evilly and brutally as possible on his toe. He screamed and yelled with pain and opened his wrist with a yank. He tossed something through that tiny space into my house near my shoe. It was likely a stone or a pebble.

I finally assailed him with the hammer but now with all my might at his toe. He yelled and screamed in agony. He pulled his leg back, and immediately I shut the door and locked it. I leaned on the door with the hammer in my hand. I lifted my hand and looked at the steel portion of the hammer. I then released my hand unconsciously. I closed my eyes, trying to remember his face.

The sharp yellow eyes.

A scar on his left cheek, just like Frankenstein has.

A bulgy nose.

Dark big lips.

The unevenly grown hair.

And a severe bald look. Which was kind of treacherous.

His spine-chilling look was molded up in my mind, and presumably not gonna forget it in my lifespan.

I straightened myself instantly and reached for the pebble. It was a greyish-black pebble, a strange one. I walked to my room and went to the window. I checked for the person. I quietly opened the window, aimed at the heavens, and threw it with all my strength. It went high up. It was downright dark. I heard the bushes move. Maybe it's the pebble. But I wouldn't bet on that as everything was swarthy, and I don't know where it went.

I quickly shut the windows down.

Later, I kept the hammer in the drawer.

I went to each room in the house to check and close all the windows and put up the curtains as I still had a bad feeling that the man standing behind the door was still probing around my house to find a way in but probably without damaging anything as if that was the case he would have effortlessly shattered the windows to break in.

When I was done, I readily went into my room, turned off the lights, and blanketed myself. Looked at the wall clock through a slight ray of light penetrating from outside the room. It was midnight, and Dad was still not home, and I realized the pool of sweat running through my hair and face.

I swept and soaked my sweat with my T-shirt. I wondered how these dangerous people like him could come to any house to rob it, then how many more people like him would still be out there in this enormous world?!'

Dangerous, corrupted, psycho, and even murderers. And if I go out, I might probably meet one or two of them. But I have decided to leave the house and can't regret it or say 'no' to my decision. I have to face all the problems that may come with my journey.

Then simply, an immediate point struck my mind. *'For what am I leaving the house?'* I gave a grin at this point. I stopped grinning and turned myself into a hefty state. I pressurized my mind into everything I could at that point. I thought back to dozens of thoughts and considered them for a while. My head hurt as I felt unsteady and clung to the bedsheets in my hands. I opened my eyes and wiped off the sweat on my forehead. I had reached a threshold. I am leaving the house because they are not my real parents, and I will find my real ones. Well, that's got a strong point.

While I was thinking about all this, a doorbell echoed in the house while I was thinking. My heartbeats rose. I got up from the bed and started walking out of the room. I was out of the hall, the main door in front. I glanced at the clock. It is thirty minutes past midnight. The man arrived about twenty minutes ago. Another doorbell echoed. I swallowed my mouthful of saliva and skulked towards the door. I reached the cabinet, took the hammer, and kept it in my pocket. I reached the door, and with a bit of courage left in my body, I opened the door while taking out the hammer from my pocket. The door swung open. I turned my head up with one eye closed and looked. It was my father! I jumped upon him with joy.

'Snap!' He snapped his fingers and said in a tone, "Hello!" I was back from the magic land. I returned to normal and smiled at what I saw in my dreams. I quickly remembered the man. I grabbed his hand and pulled him into the house. I closed and locked the door.

I was relaxed as now I could leave the house. I turned back at him and confirmed whether I pulled the man or my father. It was him. I noticed his clothes. There were some red-colored spots and marks on his pants and shirt, but instead of asking him about them, I ignored those marks and asked, "What happened? Why are you so late? It's been half past twelve?"

"Yeah, umm… it's late, and I am late 'cause our boss told me that he is lowering our salaries because he says we don't work properly." He said.

"What?" I asked.

"Yeah, and we protested against this. This took some time, and as I said before my friends and I went out to eat, and we went actually. When we reached the restaurant, it was crowded with people, and we had to wait a long time to get food." He replied with a flow. "Understand?"

"So, what happened then? Did he reduce your salary?"

"Yes, he did, and we were actually pretty sad and angry with him. He even gave me a bonus yesterday, remember?"

"Yeah!" I replied frightenedly. "What about it?"

"Nothing." He replied nervously.

"Ok, then," I gasped. "And did you get and eat the food?"

"Yes, we got the food after waiting for about thirty to forty-five minutes long. As the food was served, we ate like we had been starved for a week or two."

"And then?"

"Then what? Then… then…" he stammered.

"Then what?" I asked.

"Then… Then we came back home."

"Dad, are you hiding something? You never stammer so much."

"No, not at all." He replied like he was being exposed. "And don't ask me more questions. I am tired. Let me go to sleep."

"But."

"No ifs and buts. Go to sleep right now. Understand?"

He looked a little nervous, and sweat was leaking through his hair. Without saying anything, he turned and started walking to my room. "That's not your room," I yelled, smirking. "This is your room." I pointed to the room that was left to me.

He turned and lumbered to his room, feeling nervous and embarrassed. He closed the door.

He was looking a little different and suspicious like never before. He was acting differently, and also, he never talked or stammered like this. And his clothes, his clothes had some red-colored marks which looked fresh. And I know something might have happened out there with him on the way back home from the restaurant, and I have to find this.

It was half past one in the morning. What happened with Dad was wrong, and he is hiding something from me. This unmissable point was eating me within and giving me panic attacks. I tried not to think it over, but it went. I was in the hall sitting on the old torn sofa. After my father left his room, I went to the hall, thinking about what he was hiding. That panic attack was choking from inside. I decided to go to my father's room and find out what was happening. I rose from the sofa and walked towards my father's room. I was standing just in front of the door. Some voices were maneuvering behind the door. I put my ear on the door's rough and scratchy surface. The voices rose. Maybe he was talking on the phone. The phone was on speaker. I tried to hear and identify what was going on in the room.

"What! What are you talking about?"

"…."

"Have you Killed the boy?"

"No?"

"Why… Are you home?"

"Yeah."

"Then when?"

"Today."

Like my eyes were gone white. I moved backward, away from the door to the wall. I leaned on the wall. My heartbeats rose. My eyes grew wider. I tried to move towards the door to hear whether that was true. But can't build up the courage. Leaning on the wall, I looked at the wall cloak. It was a quarter to two. One hour and fifteen minutes to leave. Time is still left, but I couldn't risk my life with time. I changed my mind. ***I am leaving now*** for my good.

I straightened myself. Walked towards the bedroom to pick up my luggage. It was all dark. I switched on the lights. The bulb radiated the room for one last time as I reached for my backpack. I held one of its straps and hung the bag on my shoulders. Checked the money in my pocket. I had everything that I wanted except for water. I walked toward the kitchen to get a water bottle. I entered the kitchen and took the coldest bottle present at the time. I unhung the backpack and kept it on the floor.

I unzipped the chain of the bag. Tightened the bottle's cap to not leak and adjusted the bottle in overfilled accessories. I zipped the chain. And hung the backpack on my shoulder once again. I exited the kitchen and moved toward my room. I entered and checked whether I had missed anything or not. Nada. Everything was covered and kept by me inside my bag. Seeing the room for one last time, I switched off the light.

Chapter 5

I closed the door. He was still in his room. I walked ahead, brushing my hair with my fingers. That combing made shot a mini pellet of freshness in my body. I stopped. I looked around the house. Saying a final goodbye to my house. Started walking once again. I passed through the dad-turned-assassin's room and reached the entrance. The main door was just in front of my eyes. Having my eyes on the door, I realized my mother. I turned back and walked toward the cabinet where my family photo was kept. I picked it up and took out the picture from the frame. I kept it back on the cabinet. I folded the photo and kept it in my left pocket. Making a final turn in the house, I walked towards the door. I spread out my hand and held the knob. I spun the knob.

The cracking noise echoed in a big silence. Thinking he had not heard it, I pushed the door. That screeching noise was killing me, but that lasted only for a second. The door was wide open. The irritating, screeching noise stopped. I wore my pair of footwear lying near the door. I flexed my head up and gazed at the beautiful night sky. Water droplets were paddling through the air. The fog has shrouded nature. The perceptibility was zero except that white, cold, foggy, and dew nature; street lights opaqued in thickness enough to just observe a small patch of light around their heads aligned at regular intervals.

I lifted my leg and stepped on the dewy, wet grass memorizing all the happy moments I spent in this house. With a smile on my face, I kept another leg out. I was finally out in that cold-foggy nature. I turned back to close the door which I left open. I saw the house one last time and stretched out my hand. I held the knob and pulled it. That irritating screeching sound no longer feared me. I was independent and out of the house. Tears were in my eyes. But were those of grief or happiness, I can't tell right now.

I walked ahead. On that crystal-sharp grass, I walked fearlessly. Soon I was on the road. The road was unpleasantly wet. I raised my hand to see what's the time. Noticing an empty wrist, I soon remembered forgetting to wear my wristwatch (Actually, I don't have one). But I'm sure it's been around quarter past two or probably half-past two in the morning.

I continued on the road. While walking, I felt the cold breeze skim through the air. The fog formed out of my mouth and nostrils as I breathed out. My hands were cold. I rub and breathe out on my palms to maintain heat in my body. I walked and paced away from the house on the road. I was feeling hungry. But had nothing to eat. On the way, I found a bench. I was about half a mile away from the house. I decided to rest for a minute and walked towards it. I examined the bench. It was all wet. But having no choice, I sat on the bench. It was too freezing to endure. My pants became wet from behind. I no longer sat on it for over a minute and decided to move on. I stood up, and that wet pants were sticking to my skin. It was freezing and unpleasant, but I had to walk ahead without any excuses. I moved on once again.

I heard footsteps. I saw three men and a woman running on the street as they parked their vintage along the diverging road on the right. They carried weapons. I saw one tucking a Glock under his jacket. I froze at that point. Gulping and panic-struck. Sweat flowed through my hair. The only thing I was continuously mumbling was 'shit.'

I quickly walked and tried to hide behind the pole as in cartoons. But this was reality. I was spooked. I tried to peek. I saw that they were coming here on this road. I hurried and hid under the bench. They stopped and tried to sneak into a big bungalow beside me, but they didn't see me hiding under the bench. The woman climbed the wall first, and others followed except one, who stayed. He hung the gun on his shoulder, reached out for a pack of cigarettes from his pocket, and threw a cigarette in his mouth resting on his tongue. He tossed out a lighter from his jacket. It was rather an antique. I can see it was carved magnificently in an artifact and lighted the cigarette. He puffed it a few times. The smoke furled and blended in the dense mist. His face was almost obscured by the smoke. He stood there for a while as

I looked at him from under the bench. My T-shirt was drenched by the condensed mist on the bench.

At last, he smoked a perfect smoke ring and trampled it underfoot. He then climbed onto the wall into the bungalow. I heard a slight quivering among them after he jumped in.

I pushed myself to get out of there. I was stuck. I tried to push myself out, but I couldn't.

"Shit!" I exclaimed. "I have to get off here," I mumbled. I heard the gunshots from the bungalow.

"Leave everything! We have to get out of here, now!" A man shouted. One of them jumped down the window and shot at the main gate lock. Others jumped out and followed him. They all came running outside carrying guns in their hands.

One of them noticed me while running away and pointed it at me. I stared at him, baffled, waiting for my end. He put his finger on the trigger and pressed it. The woman abruptly pulled his hand up as he pushed it. The bullet hit the wall of the bungalow behind me. I was still not sure what had happened. I was back from the dead.

"Why did you do that?" The man asked. She ignored him and walked confidently to me. She bent and sat on one of her knees and inspected me. She had dark eyes and wore a damaged bulletproof suit.

"Hey, I am asking you, Chloe."

"He's just a kid," she said. "Why do you want to kill him?"

"Like we never killed a boy," he said mockingly. "He's seen us breaking into a bungalow carrying guns and killing. He's only the witness and noose for our necks here."

"Yeah, he's correct!" One of them said from behind. "He's making a point. We have to kill him. If not, we all will not see the upcoming sunlight." Another one was standing further away from this one. Quiet and observing. He was attaching a suppressor to his gun. He looked sharp and ruthless with no heart.

"I'll see, but…." He stopped. He shot him in the middle of his forehead. The bullet penetrated through his head and deflected after a spark on the pole. The blood splattered out of his head to the ground. He fell, and blood coursed on the ground. Finally, the blood flowed down the slightly slanted road and went into the drain. "You'll not!"

I broke out in a cold sweat. My heart was hammering, and my sweat broke cold. I was panic-stricken and shaking like a leaf. The other one who mocked her stood still. His mocking turned into someone's death. "What did you do, Ryker?" She astounded. "You killed another bandit this month."

"We'll get more," he said in a dark bold voice. "But why do you want to save this boy, anyway? He's the only witness and noose for our necks, Chloe." He looked at her through his sharp eyes, polishing his Glock with a napkin.

"This one's special." She turned, gave me a sportful look, thought for a while, and said confidently, "We'll take him!"

Ryker walked slowly, still polishing as he sighed to place the Glock into the dead's hand, his finger on the trigger.

"With us?!" The mocker said.

"Oh! Did I say something wrong?" she said mockingly. "Of course, we are taking him, you dumb sh-!"

"Police!" He shouted instantly. "Take him, quick!" The mocker got to me and helped me out.

"I will see you," he whispered in my ear. "You killed my friend, and now I'll kill you! You've gotten into a really bad mess."

She caught my hand, and we sprinted to escape them. We reached a three-legged intersection on the road. "Split up!" Ryker said. The other two nodded. She sprinted left, holding my hand while the other two took a right.

Two police cars drove for us, and three went to the right. She continued and made me run like hell. I miss sitting at home already! We turned for an alley, and she quickly stopped to push me into a dumpster. I resisted her call, but she pulled her gun out for my head. I jumped in for cheese like a mouse. She pushed me into the corner, my hands squishing on whatnot! Is that shit? I smelled. NOO.

She jumped in and pulled the flap. I didn't make any noise or attempt to get her caught. As I knew if she got caught, I would be sent back home and get killed by my bloodthirsty dad. So, I remained quiet.

The police drove past the alley. She peeked outside the dumpster, and so did I. All clear. There were no police nearby. "I think we should get out of here," I said softly.

"No, it's not safe out there!" She said breathily. "We have to wait for the dawn."

"Till then?" I asked immediately. "I can't wait! It's all stinky here."

"Have rest," she said. "Or go out and get caught. Just stay quiet. Don't bother me."

"Okay!" I said. I stood and tried to get off the dumpster. "If anyone's gonna get caught, that's you, not me."

"Wait! Take this," she took out her pistol and handed it to me. I grabbed it in my hand. It was heavy. She then quickly snatched the gun back and kept it back.

"What did you do?" I asked with panic.

"Nothing! I just had your fingerprints on my pistol." She grinned. "Now, if I get caught, then you'll too be the next on their list, and they will think that you were also part of this murder shit, though you were not."

"What?!" I was speechless. I slowly pulled my hand down to close the half-opened flap.

"And you know the fun part? I will tell them that you are the killer!" she laughed.

"But, what about your fingerprints? You don't have them?" She looked at me and began taking off her transparent plastic gloves, which were almost unnoticeable on her hands.

"No, I have my fingerprints, but I don't let them print on any of my stuff." I was still speechless. She pulled me down back into the dumpster by my T-shirt. "So, now you got it. We didn't do anything. You did! So, stay in here with me. You'll be safe."

"You can't blackmail me!" I said confidently.

"I am not blackmailing you, kid. I am telling you to stay with us and don't say anything to anyone about us and last night. You're part of the crime. Remember that!" she warned. "By the way, I am not as bad as you think. I never killed anyone. I am just a planner, just like the professor. I help them escape and break into a house. But don't underestimate me - I'm a black belt in Karate!" She chuckled.

"As you say!" I sighed.

It was morning. I dreamed of a perfect life where all this tragedy did not happen until my sleep broke. Then, "Hey, we gotta go!" she said.

"Go? But where?" I said. "We only went on the trip yesterday, remember?"

"Get out of your dream, kid!" she shouted. "There's no one here. It's our time. Let's go!"

"Woah!" I was back. "Okay, let's go." I hung my backpack and got down the dumpster, smelling like a dead mouse. She kept the rifle in a defective guitar bag she found last night beside the dumpster and got off. She hung it.

"Okay, so, where to go now?" I asked.

"Home." She said. She took out a small circular radar with three small red dots blinking. She pressed a rectangular button on the edge of the radar.

"What is that?" I asked. (Instead, I knew what it was!)

"Oh! I totally forgot about it!" she quickly put her hand, took a small circular case from her pocket, and opened it. There were some ant-sized balls. She took one and put it on my head, which penetrated my skin.

"What is that?" I asked. "What did you do?"

"I did nothing." She said. "Look here!" She pointed to the radar screen. A new red blinking circle emerged just beside the other dot.

"This is you," she pointed to the new dot. "This is me, and the other two dots are them." Next, she pointed to the dot beside me and the two other dots further away from us, which began moving.

"They are coming," she said. She put the radar and the case back into her pockets. Soon a car arrived and pulled over. The car was yellow and of late eighties. An antique.

"Cool!" I said, looking at the car in awe. The driver's seat window slid down to about half.

"Hop in!" Ryker said from the driving seat. The mocker was sitting back in the passenger seat, looking down at his shoes. The grief must have hit upon him hard. She dabbed the car twice and walked to keep the guitar bag in the trunk. Ryker took a gasp and bowed to lift the release button as he muttered something under his vest. She placed it in and banged down the trunk.

"Fuck!" shouted Ryker. "Every single time. She's an antique, you know that?"

"And as every time," she said, walking down to the window and squatting to look in at Ryker. "I don't fucking care."

She then sat with a straight face in the front seat beside Ryker as she slammed back the door. Ryker held onto his nerves as he closed his eyes and puffed. I opened the door and put one leg in the car. The mocker put his hand on the seat beside him where I was about to sit. "Carlos! Let him sit."

He muttered something and removed his hand.

"You said something to me?"

"Absolutely not! No way, captain." He made a face when he said, 'Captain.' I sat down on the leathered seat and slammed the door.

He ignited the engine and revved the car. "Okay, where to?" asked Ryker.

"Home," she said.

"Okay, here we go!" he said. "One hour to our destination."

On the way, looking out the window and playing country at a decent level, I zoned out.

Chapter 6

I remembered an accident. I was seven or older. It was the month of June, and summer vacations were almost at their end. I never went to school. It was Sunday, and we decided to go to a nearby park. I was too excited to go on that outing. We decided to go in the late afternoon. I spent the day loafing around, waiting for the time to pass. Finally, it was four. I danced and tapped with joy. And off we went. We all walked out of the house, and then Dad closed the door and locked it.

On the way, I held my father's hand to avoid getting lost; it also felt good. My mother was walking beside me. We reached the park earlier than I expected. The guard stopped us when we tried to enter the park through the park gate. My dad recognized the guard, and he probably did too. There was a smile on both of their faces. They shook hands and talked for several minutes. I pulled his hand to let me go and tried to get off him, but he held me tight. I almost cried until I looked at my mom as she whispered something in his ear. Dad quickly ended the conversation as it was already later than half past four on the lamp clock at the park. We entered the park, and I left my dad's hand and rushed to the slides. Dad and Mom sat on a nearby bench, asking me to take care of myself and not get hurt.

The park's key attractions were its twisted long tunnel slides and the sand area, which covered a considerably large radius at its center. People sit on its circumference as they talk and play with their children. Well, I was alone.

I played in the sand, made sandcastles, and then jumped on them. (Meet a real stupid!) I then went to the swings. I made my position third in the queue. About fifteen minutes later, someone knocked on my shoulder when I was about to swing. I turned my head back and saw there was a skinny man with somewhat curly hair. With no conversation and wording, he showed me a bar of chocolate. My eyes got fixed on the chocolate. I forgot about the swing. The man started walking backward. I also followed the chocolate. After a few minutes, the man stopped, away from my parents and the slides and the eyes of everyone. I snatched the chocolate and unwrapped it. I chewed it in my mouth and swallowed it in a few seconds of deliciousness. I fell to the ground and fainted with a whirl.

Feeling tired and sleepy with blurred eyes, I opened my left eye while rubbing the right with my fingers. Mom was sitting just beside me, holding my palm. Dad talked to someone wearing some green clothes. It was night as I peeked through the window above me, and it was a moonlit night. I stopped rubbing my eyes, and a stream of water flowed down to my ear. I kept my other palm on my mom's hand. She suddenly jumped with shock, turned her head, and looked at me.

When she saw me, she suddenly broke into tears. She wiped her tears with her fingers and leaned forward. She hugged me tightly for several minutes and kissed me thrice on my cheeks like never before, constantly mumbling that she loved me. Then, she leaned backward, scrunching her nose with an unpleasant noise. She called up my dad, wiping her tears with her hands. He stopped talking to that man and turned his head towards me. His eyes were full of tears. My mother turned her head towards him and gave him a forced courageous smile, but he didn't see it, as he just concentrated on me. He came toward me and gave me a dauntless smile. He sat on the bed near me, holding another hand. The man remained still, looking at me. Ignoring him, I looked at my father and asked him, "Where am I?"

"In the hospital," he replied.

"What happened to me?"

When I asked this question, he looked at my mother sitting next to me like… he was afraid of something to tell or know.

"What happened?" I asked again.

Still waiting for a freaking answer. They were still staring at each other as if something was wrong.

He replied, "Nothing much. Don't you care about that? The point is that you're here with us. Safe!"

He looked a little suspicious, and his eyes felt they were willing to say something so eagerly but could not. He looked backward and went off.

I looked at my mother, and she gave me a courageous smile, to which I smiled back at her. Later, she also went off.

The next morning, I woke up on another bed. Much more comfortable than the latter. I stretched myself and adjusted my pillow to comfort my back. I looked across the room. There were about twenty-three beds with people lying on them, including me. I diverted my eyes to the door. It was a man.

The same doctor I saw last night, still in his green clothes, came close to me.

"How are you feeling, lil' fella?"

"Much better. Thanks."

"What if I gave you an injection?" He grinned and asked.

I rose to my complete senses as he said injections. I looked at him with a broken voice, "But I have a phobia of injections."

"Not anymore!" He's still grinning.

I immediately looked at my hand. He removed the syringe and rubbed a piece of cotton on my skin.

Flabbergasted, I struggled to appreciate him.

"That took years of practice, my friend."

"Thanks, doc... Peter Miller."

"Welcome. But... how... how did you know-"

"The ID on your coat." I interrupted as I slightly pointed my finger.

"That's very clever of you," he said. "Maybe I should go now?"

I can make out he's impressed by me.

He turned and started walking away. His shoe taps could be heard hitting the marble floor until he left the hall.

"Hey!" A voice delivered from the bed next to me.

I turned my head. The man on the other bed next to me looked very suspicious. He had scars on his face, one eye was blue, and the other was a fake yellowish stone. He appeared dreadful. He looked at me with his horrific face and gave me a horrible smile. His one lower left Incisor was gold. I was not interested in a conversation with him, but he started one.

"Why are you here?" He asked.

"Don't know," I replied uninterestingly. "Why are you here?"

"Oh, me! Oh, I am here because a bad guy shot me just right here in my back."

He turned back, pulled over his vest, twisted his wrist, and pointed his thumb at the bullet holes. But rather than the bullet cavities, I dreaded over at the tattoos on his neck and in the center of his back. The tattoo on the neck says XO142. What's this? His car number? The tattoo on the back says *Hellicka*.

What hell's gonna lick? This makes no sense.

The man pulled on his vest, and the tattoos got covered. He turned to me, still lost somewhere.

"Hello!" he exclaimed, shrinking his eyes.

I was in the thought of all of these tattoos, especially that *Hellicka* one. "Are you lost somewhere?"

"Nowhere!" The bubble *popped* with a sudden electrifying shock. He snapped his fingers, and I was back from the fictional world.

"What's your name, anyway?" I asked. He shuffled his fingers. Looking confused or serious. (Reading his facial expressions was way more complex than a math problem)

"Ax–"

The hall gate where I was with the other twenty-three people lying on the bed opened with a *crack!*

My dad interrupted, running towards me and continuously saying something. He finally reached a point when I heard, "Hey, you got the discharge sheet."

I didn't know what it meant, but I knew it was something good.

He came to me and said, "Hey, you got the discharge sheet, lucky boy!"

"What does it mean, anyway?" I asked confusingly. That creep was still looking at me with his horrific and mysterious eyes.

"It means that you can go home now!" He replied with a massive round of excitement. I jumped into his hands. Soon the doctor (doc. Peter Miller) came and took the syringe out from my wrist. It was a little painful. Then the doctor put a piece of medical tape on the injection point.

The man behind gestured BYE with his hand fingers. I acted as if I was ignoring him, but I was not. He gave a tremendous smile while I quit the hall.

My dad had probably paid my treatment fees by taking a loan. I didn't think he had enough money for my treatment. Whatever it was, I was willing to see the *outer world* after a long *time!!*

The exit from the Hospital, and I felt free. The blue-white sky, the sun's scorching heat, the birds chirping. But after all, I'm not gonna forget that *creep*.

Never – "What the Heck?"

Thud!

Stunned at the moment. A man fell up from the Hospital to the ground just about a meter from me. Shards of glass under the body and some penetrated through. I looked up at the Hospital. One of its glasses was shattered down. A layer of blood spattered at me. His blood streamed up to my foot. His head was full of blood. His eyes opened, staring at me. He has an 'H' spelled wound scar on his forehead.

"Wait, Is it? Is it doc? Peter Miller?" I tried to look clearly at his face. "Shit!! He is!" I shouted in my mind.

I fell to the ground. Terrified. Shaking as someone stole my voice. Before I expressed anything or to shouting aloud. My mom covered my eyes with her hand, and Dad pulled me back off the crowd. My mom pulled out her hanky and wiped up my face. I started crying. Flabbergasted but could not hide it. I struggled to catch my breath. Mom hugged me, and I tried to not look as I hid under her breath.

I had never seen anything that bloody and heartbreaking. My dad held one of my hands, and my mom held another. We were heading our way home, silently and quietly.

On the way, everything was normal. The people talking, the birds chirping, and the sound of footsteps. But then the silence broke –

"It's been a long day." My father gasped.

"Yeah, it's been a real long day." My mom repeated.

I was still in shock. He was a good man of dignity and respect.

We were home. My dad unlocked the door with a *crack!* We entered the house, and Mom closed the door behind us.

Mom bent her knees and held me by my shoulders.

"Are you okay?" I asked.

"Yeah, but instead. Are you okay?" She asked with a low and worried voice.

"Yeah, what could ever happen to me," I said. "Instead, I went to the Hospital with the cause I still don't know."

She forced a laugh.

She smiled thoughtfully, "No because the incident happened before you. Are you okay after that?"

"Yeah! So, can I go to my room now?" I replied with grief but pretended to be expected.

"Go ahead." She replied.

She stood up and proceeded to Dad. I went to my room and closed the door. I sat on my bed. Intercrossed my fingers and sat straight on my bed. I closed my eyes and opened them. My cornea shrunk.

Remember the last time I saw the *late* doc Peter Miller when he was bloodily dead, and I looked up at the shattered glass? There I saw *someone!* That creep was standing about the edge of the busted glass wall of the Hospital.

He was staring at me with a straight face. I had eye-to-eye contact with him, saying something. Like there's more to come? I have seen the darkness in his eyes. He grinned and walked away, breaking the connection. And at that time, I knew if it was a Suicide or a *Murder?!* And foremost – 'Who is the murderer?'

"Maybe he isn't the murderer and doc. committed suicide. Also, the creep came to the edge to see what had happened and saw me. But sometimes it happens like – You expected and had a gut feeling for what's going to happen, but you pretend to expect the unexpected one, and the expected one happens! And I sure had a gut feeling that he's the killer."

Chapter 7

"We are here." A voice encountered. I was back with a jump. "Okay, everyone out!" Ryker said.

He stopped the car around an unfinished, multi-storied building with half-coated cement pillars holding up the three floors.

We got out of the car.

Was the project dropped, or they ran out of funding? The walls may not have been constructed as the spaces were covered with large, long blankets. It had one end nailed into the pillar, and the other was knotted to the steel rod that popped out of the pillars on the left. Sand and crushed stone piles were lying uniformly near the corner and side of the wall. Four stone piles were followed parallelly by three sand piles. Crows sat on the twisted and broken rods. The cement around them must've shredded off.

"Where are we?" I asked. "This place is awesome! I have only seen this kind of place in some movies."

"We are in Arizona about fifty miles away from Grand Canyon." She said and took a deep fresh breath.

"Arizona? How? You gotta be kidding me!"

"You passed out on the way, kid. You missed out on one hour of a whole lot of fun.

"One hour?" I was baffled by her that I almost threw on her lies. "Arizona is about two thousand miles away from Florida. It's almost a two-day drive. How is that even possible? Stop lying."

She chuckled as she gazed up at the sky, "I am not. Trust me."

"Can we go in now? The mocker said irritably.

"Who's holding you? You know how to walk." She destroyed him as she darted her eyes at him after he quarreled. "Can pull a trigger but can't stop asking for stupid permissions."

He dashed up, mumbling under his shirt. She turned a deaf ear to his scrap as he passed past her this time.

Ryker parked the car and went up the building through the stairs. She walked and went up to him, and I followed her up. We all were on the first floor.

I entered a room with no walls, as I thought. Just the floor and one partition on the side of the stairs. Two sides were covered with a blanket, and one was left uncovered for light. Shovels and steel pipes were lying in the corner.

Ryker was sitting on a chair.

"Okay, what happened with you two last night?" She asked.

"Nothing much." The mocker said. "We hid in a dumpster, as always. And at six we left."

"What? We too." I was overjoyed, like I had *hysteria!* "But we hid till nine!" He stared at me. He sighed and went away, nodding right to left and vice-versa.

"Okay, breakfast anyone?" she asked.

"Three slices of bread with some butter on it," Ryker said, unfolding a newspaper.

"Make it yourself," she said as she bit on an apple. Ryker sighed. She smiled and went away.

He unfurled the newspaper and commenced reading the first headlines. I looked at him. The way he holds and sits. He seems so brutal.

"Waste!" He yelled. "What a waste of news."

He slammed the paper on the desk. I rolled up my eyes at him. He went away to another room. I sit on the chair and put the backpack behind me. I took the newspaper. I checked the front page. The headline says:

ANOTHER MURDER THIS WEEK BY *THE ASSASSIN BREAKERS! THIS TIME AT MRS. HOLDER'S BUNGLOW!*

Mrs. Holders? I have heard that name before from my dad. Three weeks earlier, he arrived early that evening and was talking about the rumors of a wed couple in the neighborhood and how Jenna Holders, the spouse of William Holders, used marriage to cheat him of his money and then ran away and shifted across the block living in one of the most lavish bungalows in the neighborhood. The baffling argument, in this case, was that the bungalow owners were seen nowhere after her arrival on that bitter morning. The owners were a couple, and it was speculated that they were in a live-in relationship and were planning to get married in a church as they were expecting their first child. The negativity about them in the neighborhood skimmed through every house, forcing them into marriage. They were young, in their early twenties though they disappeared into nothing. Mrs. Holders was never seen leaving the house, but she was very much there. Alive. You could smell the food cooking inside, the lawn's always mowed to perfect, and loud TV volumes as you passed past her house.

I remember asking my dad during dinner how far back in time he was talking about. He replied with a cold sixteen years.

So they went into that creep house and killed Mrs. Holders? What?

There was a small box on the front page with my photo. As always, I didn't care to read the full content; however, this time, I was part of the news last night; I read the entire box as I gulped my saliva. It says:

This boy's name is Aaron Jerez. He's been missing since around three in the morning. Please inform the given number or call the police if anyone sees him. Help us to get him to his parents, Ethan and Jessica Jerez.

I grinned in disbelief. I am not returning to my parents because they do not deserve the title. I don't even know why I still call them parents; one was thirsty for my blood.

Actually two! I saw the mocker coming into the room.

"So, there you are!" He said. I kept the newspaper back on the desk. "You killed my friend."

"I did not kill your friend, understand." I got up from the chair. "You did. Maybe if you didn't have agreed to him, he might still be alive."

"I knew he was going down the second he said that," he said, coming close to my face and clutching his teeth. "I only agreed to him to have him a chance to live. I probably saved his life by mere two or three seconds, but I fucking did. Understand."

"Are you crazy?"

I moved away from his mouth. It stank worse than the dumpster last night.

"Have you seen the view up from here?" Changing the topic, he put his hand over my neck, walked to the open area, and stood on the edge of the floor. He moved a little backward while I was still on edge.

"How's the view?"

"Not that nice," I said honestly, moving slightly ahead from the edge, and I was on my heels. I put my toes on the iron rods.

"It would be better from up there." I felt a little push from behind. My foot slipped, and I lost my balance. I fell from the first floor but eventually caught one of the rods with my hand. I put another hand on another rod and made a grip. Though the rods were greased, I seized them.

"Help!" I shouted.

Mocker stood with a grumpy face.

"Lucky boy!" He said. "Help him! Chloe, Ryker."

They arrived in a fury and helped me out. They tried to pull me up. Chloe grabbed one hand, and Ryker pulled the other. I was back on the floor again.

"How did this happen?" Chloe asked, standing about a meter from me.

"Nothing, I just slipped. I was just seeing the view up from here."

"Okay." She said. "Now, never go there, okay? Come with me."

"Okay!" I said. She went away.

Ryker shot him a look and asked, "I hope you were not after this, Carlos. Are you?

"No, absolutely not!" He said.

"Good for you." He said and went away. He stared at me sharply.

"Aaron!" Her voice encountered from downstairs. I hurried down as he watched my every step until I was out of his sight.

I walked down the stairs. There were three rooms downside. Two on one side, one on the other. I was confused.

"Chloe!" I cried.

She walked out of a room, spreading butter on a brown bread resting on her palm. She waved me a hand in and went back into the room. I walked into the room. There was a multi-function thirty-five liters convection microwave oven with a stylized line pattern. A smart convertible refrigerator, a modern electric stove with four burners, an induction cooktop, and everything a rich kitchen has: a stylish sink, dishwasher, a pizza oven, a shelf for utensils, and even a meat slicer.

I was sincerely astonished and thrilled with these kitchen pieces of equipment but not the place. The kitchen was about the size of two large family-sized beds. That's a lot of space for a kitchen. The kitchen walls and floor were purely cement. The tabletop was entirely marbled.

"You like the kitchen?" she asked, buttering another bread. I looked down at the plate. She had already put butter on three slices of bread.

"Yeah!" I said, putting my hands in my pockets. "No! I was just lost in this apartment. I have never seen such big houses from the inside but just from the outside." I pulled my hands out of my pockets and put one of the hands on the tabletop, to which I reflexed immediately. It was freezing. I rubbed my forearm with another hand.

She rolled her eyes and went away, buttering the last bread. I was still in the kitchen, and she returned, giving Ryker the plate.

"What are you still doing here?" She asked as she got into the kitchen.

"Nothing," I said. "Just staying here so that I could not get lost in this place."

"Let me give you a tour of this building," she waved her hand. "So, this is the kitchen I introduced you to." She pointed to the room across the foyer before the kitchen door. "And that is the dining room."

"Can I have a look?" I walked towards the dining room. She nodded her head. I looked in. A table with a glass top and six chairs arranged around it. "Okay, next."

She then pointed to the room next to it. "It is the… um…." She thought for a while. "It is nothing, our completely useless basement. No one goes there. Let's go up!"

I had a glimpse of that room. It was utterly useless, as she stated. It seriously had nothing. Just some pieces of cement lying around.

I followed her up. She took me to the room where I first visited. "This is the devising room." She said. She pointed to the enclosure in front of the devising room entrance. There was another room. "This is the bathroom." I cast a glance. I opened the door. The walls were cemented, the basin precisely like the kitchen, a bathtub with a hand shower, and a commode.

She took me to a passageway on the same floor, following the bathroom. The walls were unpainted. We reached another room. She opened its door, and I gazed at the room. This room was painted and beautiful. I entered the room with her. The floor was wooden. "Hey, which wood is the floor of this room?" I asked.

She sat on the bed, blanketed by a pink bedcover. "Pine," She said.

I was stirring my fingers on the wall as I walked parallel to it. The walls of this room were painted blue. The ceiling was also painted blue. A chandelier was hung on the top. A small chandelier hung in the middle around a decorative stair-designed ceiling. There was a door in the room painted white with a golden knob. But I didn't peek into it.

Each wall had a LED wall lamp radiating light all-round the room. The rest of the walls were covered by framed paintings. This was the best room I had ever seen in my life.

I looked at her. She did not appear promising. I went and sat beside her. "What happened?" I asked politely.

"Nothing," she said as she shrugged her shoulders. "I don't know." She sniffs.

"Okay, I don't ask you, but you seem different in this room," I asked. "What happened here?"

"It's none of your business!" she said with a flow. I could now hear a boldness in her voice. "And I am what I am. I am not different here or whatever, okay."

"Yeah, okay," I said calmly.

She stands and walks on a soft carpet and reaches the door. "We do not have the whole day. Come on!" I got to my feet and walked to her. She closed the door.

"Okay, so this is it," she said, spreading her hand as she shrugged her shoulders. "I gave you the tour of the whole apartment."

She turned and began walking toward the stairs. "Hey, but what about the second floor?" I yelled.

She turned and gave me a sharp look and smiled. "You have got such a curious mind!" She turned and walked towards the stairs. "But sorry to say there's nothing up there. The floor is just like that room I showed you on the ground floor, completely useless, just on a large scale."

As she walked down, her voice diminished. "Money ran out. We didn't have enough money to pay the workers. So, they left. We caught one worker and constructed the stairs at gunpoint. He created the upper steps...." Her voice went off. I can't hear her anymore.

I looked at the upper stairs, an inner voice told me to go up there, but the head said to go down. I went down the stairs neglecting my inner voice. I walked down to the kitchen. She was putting cornflakes in the milk bowl. "So, is there any other bathroom? I mean, is there only one bathroom in here?" I asked her, darting my eyes to a grilled sandwich stowed on a plate beside her.

"No, the room that I just showed has a bathroom. You must've noticed the door," she said. "You want that?"

"Yeah!" I said. She must've noticed me staring at the sandwich. "What is in it?"

She picked up the sandwich and peeped between the layers of the sandwich. "It's Cheese Corn," she said. My mouth watered immediately. "You wanna have it?"

"Yeah," I said as I drooled but saved it from falling to the ground. My hands were full of saliva. She told me to wash my hands in the sink. I swabbed them thoroughly and took the plate from her.

I asked her for ketchup. She handed me the ketchup, and I squeezed it over the sandwich. I had a bite of it. It was so good even though it was hot. In a segment of seconds, I ate the whole sandwich and was licking my fingers. I made a disgusted face after I licked my fingers. "Ew!" I exclaimed. My heavenly savor was marred by a certain aftertaste. I had not even showered since I had slept in that filthy dumpster the previous night. "I have not really taken a shower; may I please?"

"Yes, sure!" She said, pointing her one hand upstairs. "You know where to go now!"

"Yes, sure I do," I said, turning back and walking up half the stairs until I realized I still had the plate in my hands. I felt stupid. I gave her an embarrassed smile as she sighed. I hurried down to the kitchen and kept the dish on the tabletop. "Foolish me!" I said as Chloe stood buttering the toast.

I climbed the rest of the steps and made a grab for the restroom. I pushed open the door and peered about. I entered and shut the door after me. "Shit!" I yelled. I opened the door and walked out; I forgot to bring my towel. I began searching for my backpack. I believe I kept my towel. I went down once more. I searched for it in every room. I peered into corners and at everything, including the beds, sofas, television, and even the dining chair. I failed to find it.

I was in such a state of anxiety when I saw a door adjacent to the stairs. On the ground floor, this was the only room that remained. I approached it and fumbled for the knob. I let myself in by opening the door. I could see nothing but blackness and the nasty scent wafting up from down there as my eyes traveled further. I took each step down, clinging onto the railings. The smell grew progressively intense as I down each step. Finally, the stench peaked at around halfway down. My eyes shot across to a toggle switch. I raised the button; it was a flickering lightbulb. A hook at the front supported a gas mask. I promptly snatched it and placed it on my face.

I took deep breaths. The odor significantly decreased. I continued to cling to the railing. The basement lightened up as if a swarm of fireflies had just materialized. I got off the bars and entered. My pupils dilated. I gaped at the bodies piled on top of each other. Their faces were so gruesomely bloodied. One of their hands was crushed, while the other's eyes were gouged out. There were blood scars all over their hands and cheeks. One was bombed in the half-head. Such a bloodbath. Dread invaded my heart. If I wanted, I could've screamed the loudest I could, but I couldn't. It was as if my voice has devoured by my heartbeats. I could hear it throbbing in my head. My cheeks were flushed with tears.

Furthermore, I did not want them to know I had just learned their most sinister secret. Tears used to stream down ceaselessly, but I managed to wipe them away as I walked to the railings shaking. I removed the gas mask and hung it up. As I ascended the stairs, I turned out the light. I carried on till I reached the foyer and fumbled for the door. I brushed away my tears and made an effort to stop them. To overcome this trauma.

I believe I've moved past it. I should leave. Fortunately, nobody noticed me leaving and returning to this room while the door was left open. My eyes swelled, and I thought my cheeks were red. Without anyone noticing, I had to ascend to the restroom. I hurried up the stairs covertly after having a glimpse into the kitchen. She was there grilling a sandwich and humming a song. It was a 90's classic, and her voice was melodious under that tough suit; I could listen to her for hours, but I was pressed for time. I sneakily ascended the stairs. I had the impression of being a top-tier burglar or a top-tier investigator doing covert work for a police force to unveil a criminal's dirty little secret. I honestly had no idea. If I didn't see Ryker coming down, I stopped halfway up. He came to a stop before I did. I dipped my head in an attempt to avoid his gaze.

Nevertheless, he ran his index finger along my chin and raised my head to face his ominous, black eyes. I started delving further after catching a brief glimpse of his gaze. My eyes began to tear up as I began to feel his suffering. His immense sorrow and even his saddest recollections.

"You didn't need to go that deeper," he said, blinking his eyes and wiping his tears which overflowed and were trying to flow out for a long time, but the barrier was strong enough to hold them. Our contact was lost somehow.

"Where are you going?" He asked.

"Up to the bathroom," I said with a flow with a lowered head. "I stayed up all night in the dumpster. I am stinking!"

He must've noticed me stealing my eyes from him. He again put his finger down my chin and raised my head. I was shaking with cold (usually it happens when you are highly nervous or afraid), and my limbs went numb.

"Why are your eyes swollen?" He asked. I was still shivering but answered.

"I- I didn't sleep well last night, probably because of that." I stammered badly. "Maybe if I have a bath, I could feel better!"

"All right, go!" he said, leading me up. I walked up gently, holding on to the railings. I eventually made it to the floor. I took a stroll to the restroom. I entered the bathroom and then turned to lock the door. I spotted my backpack resting on a chair in the devising room. I flung the door open and reached for my backpack. I was hugging my backpack so tightly that I failed to see the mocker on the desk.

"See, see. Who's here?" the mocker mocked. "You killed my pal and this time ate my sandwich! You really are a noose to our heads."

"I had no idea it was your sandwich," I explained. "And if I had known, I wouldn't have eaten that shit."

"What did you just say?" He asked bluntly. I rushed to the restroom, hugging my bag as he dashed himself with all he had to chase me, but I got into the bathroom and locked it. He banged the door violently for the next few minutes of fury.

Eventually, he stopped hammering on the door and must've left, but I couldn't risk it. I then had a shower. I shampooed my hair for the first time in a while; and cleansed my skin with a hundred-dollar body shower gel, the most expensive thing I'd ever used. I considered the corpses lying there as I was in the shower. Every time I think about it, my heart sinks. I can't continue to live here, not just because of the corpses but also due to him. He seems a potential threat and not inclined for a truce. These factors summed up as they propelled me to drive an escape from the house.

The moment I was done, I dried myself off with a towel before pulling out my T-shirt and slacks from the bag. I had no alternative but to keep my damp towel inside the backpack. I drove my fingers to comb my slightly damp hair. I then rubbed my moist hand on my pants. I put on my shoes and socks, which I had stashed in my backpack, to avoid getting wet. I went to the door after I hung my backpack that leaned against the wall. I pushed open the door a half-inch and peered through the crack. I looked around meticulously. He was outside the line of vision. I quietly closed the door after slipping out of the restroom. I caught a glimpse into the devising room. Ryker leaned back in the chair, sipping on an old-fashioned mug. The mocker likewise seated in front of him. They most likely were in a conversation, discussing something.

"None of my business!" I scoffed. I simply need to leave without anyone noticing.

I walked downstairs, pretending to be expected. Soon I was on the ground floor. Just a few steps, and I am out here. I walked to the door and opened it.

"Where are you going?" A voice encountered. I was frozen to death.

I turned around as a warrior of words sent to war and lied with my might, "Nowhere, just going out for a walk."

"No, just stay in here!" she said.

"Why?" I spurred out a microsecond after she denied it. My heart pounded as it sank before a storm could perform its action. My nervous system automatically broke my knuckles as I wiped the sweat off my hands to my pants. "Why can't I go out?"

"You know, last night, a man was killed!" She said nonchalantly. "And the fun part, we killed him! So just stay in here."

"Okay," I replied. But whatever she made me understand meant nothing to me now. I'll still leave the house.

She turned and went upstairs. I turned and moved out. The crushed stones crunched as I placed my foot on the uneven gravel. I closed the door, and this time this door didn't make any cracking noise. *I think I am getting better at this!*

I finally made it across the dirt and was out. I could only perceive the road as far as my eyes stretched. Nothing more. I gaped and shook my head in disbelief at what was happening in my life. Yet I had to move and walk. I exhaled and started to go forward with all of my enthusiastic fervor.

I struggled as I trudged into this desolate landscape for around thirty minutes. I took frequent watchful turns to see whether they were following me. The abandoned property was still visible, and the road was long and unswerving. I had not anticipated this winter in December. I was exhausted, and short breaths were about to kick in. I turned around once I understood that it was a poor decision and that I had been safe with them. I noticed a pale figure standing outside the site's fences. I recognized Ryker right away. I started to retrace my steps on the freeway. With his hand directly facing me, the figure moved into view. The shot's reverberation ringed the valley of strewn cactuses.

Fortunately, the bullet missed me and dissipated in the air.

I froze. Why the hell did he shoot at me? Does he not want me back? Has he joined forces with that mocker? They are a team, of course!

Two figures appeared behind him. They were armed. They were perplexed and seemed to be interrogating him extensively. He walked back in. One of them pointed his finger at me and yelled. The slight echo almost struck my ear. The other shadow gazed at me and remained still. Looking at me intently. I immediately made a U-turn and started walking. As I stared back, one figure surged while the other stayed frozen.

My cheeks and fingers twitched as the adrenaline surged through me as I hurried. I continued to walk till late in the afternoon. Hopefully, they did not come after me. The house faded away about five hours ago. Hundreds of vehicles passed by this begging fellow asking for a lift, but none made an effort to rethink the humane laws of humanity to help a stranded kid. After a few more passes of dead humanity, I saw a trailer approaching.

I walked to the center of the road and waved my hand to the trailer this time. No matter how dead humanity is, they will stop if the driver in the seat holding onto the steering and controlling the acceleration with his feet is not asleep.

The trailer stopped by and pulled over. He slid the side glass down to half and with his hand out the window.

"Where do you want to go, kid?"

He was a half-balded man. He wore a cap, a red-white checks shirt, and an incredible brown leather jacket.

"Phoenix," I said, looking up at him.

"I am going to Tucson," he said. "Hop in, and I'll drop you."

I went crazy. Finally, a spare of humanity! I quickly got in the truck and accelerated. The cool air in the trailer made me feel better, a lot better. I was feeling so relieved. I was so happy. He seemed to be a nice guy, so I wanted to be frank with him. "So, how long have you been working?" I asked.

"Oh, you mean this!?" he exclaimed. "Six years, actually. Or more than that." He grinned.

"So, what are you doing on this road, you know, alone?" he asked.

"Oh, me!?" I exclaimed. "I got lost from my parents in Grand Canyon, so I decided to move home, you know. When they come home, they'll get me."

"That's sarcastic." He said. "The starting and ending part was, the rest was totally okay."

"Oh, no, no-"

"Oh, yeah, yeah. I got it!" He interrupted.

"No, I didn't mean that. Maybe our both speaking styles are the same!" I said.

"Oh, man. I got it." He said.

After a few minutes of silence, we broke into laughter. We talked for hours then. I also slept in the truck for hours. Whenever my sleep broke, I saw him smoking a cigarette. But you can't judge a person on that.

"Hey, hey! Wake up." He shouted. "You need to wake up." My eyes were blurry. I looked around. It seemed to be an emergency. I must've blinked a couple of times to see clearly.

I looked out of the window. It was evening twilight. The sky was shining in colors I had never seen.

But the question was, will I ever be able to see it again?

For that instant, my answer was *No*.

"Where am I?"

"About halfway to Phoenix." He said, stuttering.

"Then, why did you stop the trailer?" I doubted. And also, he doesn't seem well. He was holding up to steering and staring imprecisely to the front. Sweat was flowing down his cheeks and dripping to his seat. "Hey, I asked you something?"

He was not replying to me. He was unconsciously looking in front as he was searching for something. I must've asked him dozens of questions, but he ignored me the whole time. And I also couldn't make out why he woke me up, for no reason, I think.

"He's here!" he mumbled. He looked stressed and hopeful. He was staring at a white trailer about double ours. He waved a hand out of the window, which was already open. The trailer blinked its headlights. He got off the trailer. I was absolutely blank about what was happening.

He walked to the other side of the trailer and pushed the gate open. I asked him, "What was happening?" several times, but he ignored it every time. He grabbed the duct tape and cut a piece of it. He headed his hands with tape in his fingers. I understood what he was up to. I tried to defend myself, but my hands weren't moving. I looked imprecisely around the buckles of the seatbelt. I noticed I was handcuffed to a trailer rod and could not move. I jerked my hands to try to get rid of it, but I couldn't. I also got a scratch on my wrist. I was also seat belted. I struggled not to get taped, but he punched me above the abdomen. I grunted. He then smacked me in the same place twice. Blood dripped through my mouth. I was tired. My energy vamoosed me. He quickly double-tapped my mouth. I was not able to move even a little bit. I turned my face to him. He looked out. He seemed afraid. His eyes widened. He quickly closed the gate and hurried to the other side of the trailer. He, too, had trouble running. He got up to the driving seat and drove to the white trailer.

He reached the trailer and pulled over. He got off and came for me again. He deplumed the gate and threw it on the road. He put his hand under the seat, grunting and exterminating the seat, along with me sitting on it and holding it like a football. He carried it with me, sitting and reaching for the white trailer's door. He opened it and threw me into it. He closed the door and probably went away. It was all dark in there. I could feel the surface beneath me. My head was in contact with the trailer. I heard the engine roar. He must've revved up the trailer. I could feel the increasing difference between me and the ground beneath the trailer. I was feeling lighter, and soon I started moving and crashing. I moved randomly around all sides of the cartesian plane. It was too dark to see anything in. I was trying to grab something to hold onto, but nothing came my way. It was completely empty, and all did was slip my hands on the metal to find a grip. It was too smooth. I was sometimes floating and then crashing onto the trailer again. My pain receptors died that day. I felt everything everywhere so badly that they now felt nothing. About every bone in my body was broken and crushed to pieces. I was shouting about pain, fear, everything. And I got a final smack on my head, and I probably died.

Later, I woke up. I was feeling heavy and had a slight headache seizing my head. I put my hand on my head and helped with some massage. I opened my eyes. I looked around and searched for a bottle. I grabbed the bottle and took a sip. The pain soothed. I got up from the bed and stood still. I rubbed my eyes and yawned. I walked to the mirror. My eyes widened and literally fell out. I screamed. My eyes were rolling onto the ground, but I could see it. I cried and ran everywhere, but there was no one. But I can see even after both my eyes popped out, and I probably stepped and crushed one of them under my leg! I screamed!

I am on a bench.

Lying on the bench with a slight headache, I woke up. I turned my eyes and looked about everywhere. I stood up, and my clothes were all sticking to my skin. I was cold. It was unbearably unpleasant. I turned my upper body backward to see. It was all wet. I even put my hand behind my back to find my T-Shirt totally soaked. It was not until I entirely became conscious. I looked everywhere.

It was the same bench I sat on to give myself a little rest. And also, the same place! I looked up at the bungalow. The glass wasn't shattered. Another thought struck my mind. I had a complete look at myself. I checked my eyes. Well, I feel them. Although, about every bone of my body hurts. I checked my clothes. It was the same clothes I wore in my so-called dream, which I now named: The Apartment. That means all I watched and did was just a dream! The mocker, the driver, and Chloe were all just a dream?! Well, I don't think so. It felt so real!

And also the eye-popping one. That was absolutely a dream. I can bet on that! (again, checking both of my eyes). This means I saw a dream about myself within a dream! Ain't that cool, huh?

I unzipped my backpack resting on the bench, which was dampened from one side. I checked the old clothes I had worn earlier (according to the dream). They still stink. They were stinking badly. I zipped back my backpack.

I think I must've started doing actions from the dream in real-life! Although it made no sense, I needed a reason to convince myself that it was indeed a dream. I stretched out my hand to reach for the backpack. I grabbed one of its straps but noticed a small scratched scar on my wrist. I pulled it and hung it on my shoulders. I positioned my hand on my chest level and noticed my wrist. The scrape on my wrist was certainly a scratch. And it was a big deal as I didn't even have a scratch or scar on my body. So, where did it come from? Also, the mark appeared fresh. And as far as I remember, I saw this mark in my dream. I was absolutely not sure what was happening, but I let it go, although all the clues darted to a single point- The dream, The Apartment, while some did not. Considering everything and happenings as a dream, I decided to move on.

I sighed, "Better it be a dream!"

Chapter 8

It was morning. People walked across roads and footpaths, accelerating the automobiles running on the streets. I walked about five miles continuously, and my legs were about to faint. I rested for a while on the roadside bench. I unhung my backpack and unzipped it. I searched for my water bottle but sensed a tricky sort of thing. I grabbed it and took it out with my fingers wrapping it. I opened my wrist. It was the pebble.

I was confused. "How did it come in here?" I questioned myself. I had thrown it out in the bushes, as I remember. There was really something wrong with this pebble. I scanned the pebble. I figured out a small bump on the top of its smooth and glossy surface. I put my finger on it.

"What the Heck?" I yelled as a woman crashed into me. I turned to her, and she spilled her double chocolate crème Frappuccino on my pants. (It was written on the cup!)

"I'm really sorry! Actually, I was on a crucial call with my boss." She apologized to me.

She was a tanned woman and seemed to be Asian. She had blonde colored hair and wore a summer crop top T-shirt under a red leather jacket and a pair of jeans.

"But what I'm gonna wear? That's my only pants."

"Don't worry! I'll buy you a new one. Come on." She took me to a nearby store to buy me new pants. Really, that first experience of that cool breeze of the air conditioner was overwhelming.

I quickly went and chose my new polka-dotted black pants.

"Zzzzzz!" Her phone rang up. It's from her boss. She told me to wear these pants in the trial room and received the call.

I looked like a clown. I went and tried on some more expensive new pants. I called help from a volunteer and tried some more. I finally locked eyes on a pair of blue pants with knee pockets and wore my new pants in the trial room as told and took all my belongings from the old pants and kept them in the new pocket. I, too, kept that pebble in my pocket.

When I was done, I kept my old pants in my bag and opened the door. I went to her. She's still talking on the phone. Her phone was a little loud:

"Send me a photo of him." She told.

"Okay! I will. But the pic will take longer to download. It's of high resolution. Find him soon, Sara." Her boss said.

"Okay, boss! I'll find him." She replied and hung up the phone.

"So, your name's Sara." Your phone was a little loud.

She looked at me and said, "Yup! Are you done? Let's go now. I have work to do."

"Okay, let's go," I replied with a smile.

In a minute, we were out. There was hardly anyone on the footpath at this time. She looked at me and asked for a goodbye.

"Okay then, bye." She said.

"Hope we meet again!" I gasped.

She turned and continued to walk. I waited for twenty seconds and started following her. I followed her quietly for about ten and then another twenty minutes until I crashed into a big fat, about a six-and-a-half-feet-tall man. I bounced back and fell back to the ground.

"I am sorry." I apologized. But instead of forgiving me, he pulled me up and threw me back to the ground. I grunted, "Hey, I said sorry!"

But he was in no mood. He stood still and walked away, murmuring.

I moved out as quickly as I could. The big fat walked away, reacting weirdly just like those weirdos. I looked at Sara. She was far away, turning left. I sprinted as fast as I could toward her. She turned left to the road. Within ten seconds, I was there. I turned left. I saw her. I caught her up. I tapped her shoulder. She turned back and asked me, "What are you doing here?"

"Nothing. I am just here to help you with your mission."

"No, I'm fine. I can do it myself." She said.

"Please, wh-" Her phone wrapped around her fingers, and she received a message. She checked her phone and looked at me.

She quickly covered my mouth with her fingers and forcibly took me into the alley. She threw a metal ball at the entrance of the alley. It was created like a liquid crystal display.

"Shh," she repeated continuously. I bit her on the fingers. She shouted with pain. She took her hands off my mouth.

"Help! Help!" I cried. I prepared to run. But she caught me by my T-shirt. I heard my collar tear. I could listen to the edge of my collar ripping.

"Wait, I'm here to help you. I mean no harm!" She said. But I overheard her and tried to get away.

"Hey, stop! Otherwise, I have to try another way." She said. I still overheard her. At the time, I was just hoping to get away from her and her.

"Stop! You left me no choice. I'm sorry it had to be in this way." She crossed her right leg ahead and pushed me to the ground by pulling my left leg. She then pounded me hard on the head with her elbow twice. I was hardly crying for help.

The last thing I remember is being knocked down in the alley. My eyes were blurry. I was reclined on a soft, comfortable bed. I could see a woman cooking in the kitchen, looking up at the ceiling fan circling above me, the yellow light of the lamp.

I had an adventurous dream about leaving the house and of the pebble.

I must've woken up several times but assumed it was a dream, so I just passed out again. The next time I woke up, I remember being spoon-fed by someone that tasted like chocolate ice cream.

"Welcome back!" She greeted. She must've seen my eyes open. Dripping the ice cream on my chin.

"Where the Heck am I?" I got off the bed and wiped the ice cream with my T-shirt, which dripped off my chin. I took a beer bottle kept near the bed and held it by its neck, hitting it with the four-drawer cabinet to have a sharp-edged oar.

"Hey! Easy boy, easy." She said. "You're still not in good condition. Come back to bed and keep that thing away."

"No!" I said. "I will not unless you tell me what's happening here."

"Okay then, I'll tell you." She said, getting low. "But just be careful with that thing. It can hurt you badly."

"Stop caring for me!" I shouted. "Just tell me what the hell is going on."

"But just don't interrupt. Okay!" She continued –

"Years back, about millions of light-years away from K-10, there's XO142 at the outer edge of a galaxy, what we call Messier 31. XO142 is approximately double in the earth's size and mass."

"Wait, what?" I asked, disagreeing. "What's K-8-9?"

"K-10." She said with a flow nodding her head.

"Yeah, what's that?"

"A planet." She said. "All questions at the end, boy."

"Okay, continue. I just want to know what the hell is going on?"

"I know. The last few days had been tough on you."

"How do you know that?"

"I know much more about you than you do about yourself, kid."

"How?"

"All the questions at the end!" she said. "You wanna listen or not?"

"Okay, go on!" She continued-

"The planet was quite happy and satisfied with its needs. Has a Type I civilization and two moons – Gah and Beka and is currently working on building an artificial moon.

Its population is approximate to the earth. There are eleven huge landmasses, and each landmass has a capacity of forty-five nations, each ruled by a single king. The rest is covered with a shallow layer of water about five-ten feet deep.

You can call XO142 a destined planet. Whoever born, there is being destined to do something. Each king to a farmer, even a foe to a best friend, everything is fated! You can't tell where you're destined to be, but you'll reach it. Counting on your faith and loyalty towards it, you can either reach your destiny in your sixties or even in your twenties.

After every decade, ten warriors are born in each nation, destined to kill the king to acquire the throne. From childhood, they are trained. When the master announces they are ready, the warriors and the king fight. All ten versus one. Whoever kills the king gets the throne. The master who trains is ancient. No one has seen him in centuries except the decade warriors. It's always in the rumor that he's been alive from the beginning of this world's evolution. One of the first men. The funny part is no one talks about him because no one knows anything about him."

I was chewing my nails and got lost in those imaginary worlds she had just discussed.

"Well, that's bullshit!" I said. "See, I never went to school. I am illiterate. That doesn't mean I am a fool, you understand?"

"That's not bullshit, kid." She said. "You have to believe me!"

"See, if you want to just trouble me, waste my time, or make fun of my situation, then say it." I mocked. "I have work to do."

"You're pathetic!" She caught her head and sat back on the edge of the bed. "Just go!"

"What? Did you just ask me to leave?" I mocked her. "Okay, anyway, I have to go and search for my real mother."

"What did you just say?" She asked instantly.

"Excuse me?" I asked her pardon. She stood up, walked toward me slowly, and stood beside me.

Spelling every word of that sentence carefully, she repeated, "What did you just say?"

"…Um… I have to go and find my real mother?"

"Oh, Mother of Kohb!" She exclaimed, turning her back against me. "I know your mother!"

"Uh… and why would I believe you?" I turned and got to the main door.

"You have to believe me, kid." She said pleadingly. "Look up in my eyes." She started moving towards me, staring precisely into my eyes.

I just can't look away! She was getting closer every second. I just needed to break the contact. I placed the broken neck of the bottle, breaking contact with her eyes, and she blinked and fell to the ground. I opened the door with shrunk iris and walked out. I rolled my eyes and had a glimpse of her room door painted brown with three white stripes on it and deeply scratched. I looked down the stairs. I was two stories up. I hurried down.

I was sitting on a bench holding up to a rusty street night lamp, and its moisture dampened my hands.

I looked around. I saw kids, not just more than three or five, walking with their parents holding up their fingers. I could recall the same with my stepparents. I used to grab their fingers and walk around. Wherever I pulled them, they followed me. It was too nice of them to adopt a kid who's not their blood. I snuffled a little and looked back.

I got up and hurried back to her, climbing up the stairs. I remembered the brown door with strips on it, but every door was the same.

"Shit," I tried to think harder. "It was scratched!"

I began searching for the door mumbling it continuously. Reaching every door, I scrutinized it. "Got it!"

I knocked on the door. It swung open, cracking. The noise hurt me badly, and I got a quick headache. As the door rested, the pain faded away in an instant. I moved in. There was she reclined on the wall. She stared at me with a glance of hope and asked, scowling, "Changes of mind?"

"No, Just here for my backpack. I left it here."

She threw the bag at me, which directly hit my face as her only brick of hope shattered into pieces.

"Nice shot," I said, picking up my bag. "I would recommend you to see a psychiatrist."

"She sighed and said in a low tone, "Just go. It was a mistake!"

I felt terrible for her. 'Though she sounds crazy, whatever has been happening with me in the last few days is no joke. Those dream-like happenings, the farmers, the restaurant, and even abandoning my house. Everything's changed in the last few days. I am not what I was before.' I spoke to myself.

I walked to her to say, "Sorry." I sat on my knees and gently kept my hand on hers.

She quickly opened her eyes and hurtled to the door. She locked the door. "Get down," she said.

"Why?" I asked. "I am very vexed with you!"

"I am sensing something wrong," She said, stealthily moving to the kitchen. "Get down!" She pointed her finger down the bed.

"You know what? I am done with you." I said, getting up and hanging my bag. "I gotta…"

"Where you are, princess?" Someone behind the door interrupted. I quickly crouched behind the bed. She grabbed the knife block containing approximately seven knives and carried three more in her hands.

Someone behind the door banged the door with a sudden and low-pitched voice that came up, "You in there?" I can hear them sniggering outside the door. Yes, there are more of them outside by the door. Their sniggers were evident enough to say that there are more than ten outside. There was another big thud on the door that barely made a small crack on the door. I quickly went prone under my bed without a second delay. The space here was so less that I struggled the first time in. I turned my eyes up and looked for her. Another big thump on the door was louder and more robust than the former. I can see a deep crack splitting the door into more than five huge lamp-size pieces. I struggled out my upper body and unhung the bag. I moved in again swiftly and pulled my bag in.

I unzipped it and began searching for any kind of sharp tool which could be used as a weapon. I came across nothing but a ball-pointed pen.

"What am I going to do with it?" I questioned myself. I sighed as I couldn't believe my unbelievable luck!

I held the pen on my wrist to stab a person with it.

There was another loud thump on the door. Their huge laughs were briefly audible. "We're coming in now, babe." A man said, laughing louder than before.

And now, there was silence. A heart-pumping silence. My heartbeats were going louder and faster. The beats were echoing in my body until I heard a loud gunshot. My heart popped into my mouth, and my eardrums went numb. I jerked it a few times until I saw the door blow up. I tried to cover myself with my forearms. Some blown-up pieces of wood and almost almond-sized splinters got penetrated my arms. I grunted and then screamed with pain. Blood spluttered out and dripped down to the floor, staining it red. I gazed towards the door through my watery eyes. It was smoggy and dusty, both at the same time. Soon my T-shirt got red-stained and got gummed to my chest. I started plucking out those splinters and wooden pieces though I could barely see amidst the chaos through those saturated pairs of eyeballs. I blinked. Tears flowed down my cheeks. I groaned and sometimes squeaked every time I plucked a splinter. It's the heart-pumping dare you can ever give to your friend.

Soon I heard the footsteps of a few people walking in. I heard someone move from my left. I darted my eyes to the left. I almost forgot that Psycho was still in there…

She slowly eased out a glossy knife from that wooden block, enough to reflect your face in it but at the same time as sharp as a Katana. She looked at me with gorgeous kind eyes, slowly put her finger on her lips, and shushed me. I was brought to stillness. Staring at her, she took her fingers off the lips and threw the knife straight away she had been holding for almost thirty seconds. Blood squirted out of one's head and fell to the ground. They began shooting randomly everywhere, and she started throwing knives into that smog. Everything in the room got destroyed and turned into huge splinters and sawdust. All windows blew up and cracked into smaller shards that, too, got into my feet. I screamed, and blood spattered out my feet. I grabbed those shards with my toes and tried to pull them out. I could feel the blood flowing rapidly down to the floor. I was in terrible pain. I pulled all the shards out. Their sharp edges must've made several deep or slight cuts on my toes. I could feel the skin cut in half with my index toe fingers. I was in great pain, and it will haunt me for years.

I heard a shout from my left.

One shot got her to the ground, hitting her left thigh and burning red hot. She yelled and screamed in pain. Grunting, she went to the wooden block and continued throwing, although they weren't thrown hard enough to penetrate through them. They stopped firing.

Some blue fluid thing slowly flowed down to me. It looks dense and viscous. It smells terrible. It reached out to my hands and mixed up with my blood, forming a purplish-red hue. It smells even more disgusting. I got my T-shirt stained with it. My T-shirt's a mess now!

The smog puffed back and got sucked into a metal ball. The shooters were armored in heavily equipped and Technologized suits with Android arms emitting red rays through three curved rectangles aligned straight above the elbow on the upper limbs of the half-vacuumed gloved suit, followed by two yellow parallel strips painted down the shoulders on either side extending to wrist bones.

The ball was clasped on a shooter's fingers, and all the smog got sucked up in it. The red light turned green when the smog got collected into three holes, drilled into it, and clinked. The three openings closed with three cylinder-shaped structures above the openings held by several tiny needles on the circumference of those openings, which drilled down and sealed it tight, making it look like a perfect sphere ball. The metal ball was undoubtedly the size of a baseball.

Their faces were concealed under a head Armor of the same material as the whole body with a small triangle-shaped black glass in front of them. One of their glasses slid up, revealing their most anticipated faces. He was my father. His eyes were fixed on the ball. A long blue scar on his face which looked pretty fresh was gleaming on his face. He sighed and aimed the ball at his heart. A small round opening unlocked the suit, and the ball fitted in completely. He looked around. He nodded and signaled his crewmate standing vigilantly right to him with some cool-looking gun growing out of after his elbow. It walked to her and pointed its gun at her head. She was prone and bleeding badly. She was out of knives and must've missed those throws after being shot. She turned her head to me and stretched out her trembling hand. I felt something deep within that moment – a *connection!*

He looked at her and smirked. He nodded to his crewmate standing left of him. He walked to the bed under which I was prone and returned to my foot side, crushing shards on the floor. I tried to pull in my legs, and fortunately, it did, but I was stuck there. He put his hand under the bed and threw it to the other side. There was absolutely no place left to hide, but it won't matter now. I thought that I was gonna die, but I didn't. He grabbed my back collar and pulled me up at gunpoint. He threw and swamped me on my knees before my father, with my head facing downwards. I slowly turned my head left to see her. Her eyes were closed. Tears dropped down to the floor.

"Is she-" I turned back, my head only watching his boots.

"Dead?" He interrupted. "No, she isn't. She's just resting. She has only lost consciousness for now, and so do you!"

He slapped me hard, and I fell to the ground, splattering blood from my mouth.

Chapter 9

The last thing I remember was being slapped after a shootout and falling to the ground, where I discovered two men lying dead with a knife in their heads, leaking some blue liquid out of their bodies, flowing bafflingly to me. It was so strange. I believe it has to be some kind of oil or lubricant, but it doesn't look like one. If it's flowing from the head, it has to be blood. You can't just store oil in your head armor; In addition, the liquid was in a considerable amount as it was constantly leaking out.

But how can the blood be blue?

I rolled my eyelids up. All I could see was white and flashy. I struggled to sit. My head feels heavy. I got up on my feet but fell. I swept myself to the washbowl and struggled to uphold tightly to it. I feel exhausted. I look up in the mirror. Blood that flowed from the mouth had dried up and stuck to the skin. Either side of my cheek has been swollen up red. My hair was a mess. Instead, I was a mess. I ran the tap and washed my face. I could not believe how, but I swept my face with my T-shirt, damped in dry blood. It smelled terrible, and I washed my face once more. This time, I let it dry off on its own. I was in a room.

Lights beaming through walls. In fact, it appears that the walls were the lights. The floor was also radiating energy which was almost making me blind. I covered my eyes, and the lights went dim. Perfect. It was now soothing to the eyes.

I looked towards an energy shield rushing with a slight buzzing. Tiny pyramidal projectors aligned vertically downwards stuck to both sides' walls casting the shield. There were dozens of them aligned casting.

The barrier disintegrated and faded away. A guard walked in. He was wearing a techy muscled black armor. He walked to me, holding another techy rifle blaster, and stood beside me.

"Get up!" He ordered. His cranky voice almost made me jump.

I stood up. Although I was in no condition to walk. My foot was all cut. The skin was peeling off with flesh. My legs were gone pale blue below the knees, and blood was not splattering out through gashes.

"Follow me."

I tried walking but failed to. I fell back to the floor. The guard turned and gave me a nibble of his gun. He electroshocked me hard. I was fluttering. He ordered me to get up once again.

When he noticed I couldn't, he spoke something with his forearm near his face. That must be a transmitter built in there. Two men came down and picked me up. The two followed him. The place was junk, and rust had almost flooded the entire walls. Sewage pipes ran through the walls as one of the pipes might have leaked all over. We passed through a narrow passage that widened up.

They were walking up then, carrying me behind. Soon, the pipes took a turn, and I found myself in a vast hall. Later I found myself in front of a small cabin. The two took me there and made me stand in a queue. A queue of all weirdly dressed humans. I didn't know if it was Halloween.

Out of nowhere, I shouted, "Happy Halloween!"

They all turned and looked at me with scornful eyes.

A man with tennis-ball-sized eyeballs.

Football-sized head

Little to no nose, just two holes above the lips.

Smallmouth about two centimeters.

About everyone in there looked similar to that guy. He mumbled something and looked away. I wanted to ask why, but I didn't want to face that dreaded face again.

Water dripped off the ceiling with a constant interval to the ground. Leaked water then created the way and streamed down the circular canal at the center of the hall, which explained the tilt towards the center of the floor at all sides. The area is too rusted and was no different from the passage we walked through.

When I was next in the queue, it struck me that I wasn't told what to do. What do I have to do?

Oh, yeah! Got it.

When I was called by another cranky voice, I walked forward.

"Trick or Treat?" I asked with a wide fake grin.

"This is not your Earthly Halloween, young boy!" She exclaimed in her similar cranky voice as his. "Stretch your hand here."

She put out her gluey jelly limb from under the cabin and pulled my hand near the counter. My hand was soaked with a gluey and viscous fluid. It had a strange, pleasant smell. One that could make you fly in the clouds, and I did fly but was back to consciousness when I realized what had happened. I was terrified.

"What was that?"

"What's what?" She chuckled. "Oh, that? That's my limb. I had five, but two were cut down in a war."

"Wh- What War?" I was stammering insanely. My hands were trembling, and I couldn't do any better.

"You, young boy! I shouldn't have done and told you that." She said, handing over to me some pills soaking wet. It was slimy and sticky. "It's my fault. You are new here."

I was out of words, but I had questions. My speech was triggered next after my whole body started trembling. I could not ask but stammer. The two took me to the nearest table. The guard followed and asked me to swallow the pills.

"Swallow the pills she just handed over to you. Be sure, only swallow, no chewing!" He warned sternly. "If you, you'll have to suffer major consequences!"

I looked over at it. It was so unpleasant and gross. The more I looked at it, the more disgusting it got.

"Eat it, now!" He activated his gun, and the buzzing was way much louder to me than to him. "The substance will work as a digestive fluid and will help resist its adverse effects. Also, it works as lubricate while taking pills."

I closed my eyes and filled my mouth with those. I swallowed the pills first, then the material. It felt like I would throw up, but I drank it anyway. It was slimy. Almost similar to aloe vera.

"Good."

They held me up. Walked. A place I am not so familiar with. They took me back behind that barrier inside that four-walled room.

They threw me in. I mean, they threw me in!

They swung me and threw me like a bag. I got my head bumped hard to the ground and went blank for a minute or two, and they enjoyed it from behind that barrier. No voice was coming through, but the guard must've given them orders to stay and guard the barrier.

They must've refused to do so and eventually got electrocuted by him. They trembled on the ground while he threw a small pistol blaster at them (which I found out later.)

He walked away. When the two got to their senses, they both stood up and picked up the guns. One of them hovered his fingers over the barrier, and some options appeared over it. He must've adjusted the transparency settings. The barrier grew dimmer every second until I could only see undetailed figures and no faces.

Chapter 10

It had been several days since I ended up here. Every day I woke up and freshened up in the right corner of that room. I have nothing to do but wait for them to give me those pills and back here again twice a day. I remained unknown, and my brain must've lost its senses to identify what part of the day or time it was. Mostly, the room radiated light twenty-four by seven, but it always remained orangish dark behind the barrier. I was slowly growing crazy as time passed.

I was losing hope of ever getting out and began believing I would die here hopelessly. Tears were flowing down, which later turned me to sob.

The guard came in. He asked me to get up. I didn't. I heard the buzz of that gun activating, and he moved towards me.

"Don't! I am getting up. Give me a second. You don't have flesh coming out of your toes." I spoke.

Although my feet were getting better and healed faster than I thought, fresh flesh had almost expunged the older skin.

He backed off and deactivated the gun as the buzzing went off. And then, for the first time in a while, I did not get electrocuted.

I struggled to stand upright. I looked at him with my damp red eyes.

"You have been called by our Head Commander. You better hurry." He ordered.

"I don't want to go."

"That attitude does not work here, kid. Now, walk!"

"No, I don't want to."

He activated it and electroshocked me, and I fell back to the floor. He ordered the two to hold me up and follow him. They took me to a cabin reading '***THE HEAD COMMANDER'*** under a patch of light dust but not in the language I knew. But I could read and understand it.

I didn't know what was happening to me.

How could I read and understand those that had happened to me before?!

He pressed some keys on the keypad beside the door, and the metal doors slid open. It was in awful condition. Thick wires dangling out of the ceiling, going naked at their ends.

They made me sit on the metalline floor with mesh on some parts. The door was opened and was just behind my back. The guard went on to a circular desk positioned in the center. He pressed some buttons, leveled up the controls, and swiped his fingers on many screens. The two were standing beside the door, giggling and whispering.

"Losers," I mumbled.

He placed a projector on the desk and was cabling to a source. He was not able to plug cables into the socket. His hands were trembling, and he could not do any better. He seemed to be afraid of something. I hadn't seen him like that. Maybe he's just a coward behind those tough suits. After a while, he faced the projector before me and pressed a button on the screen. He came and stood beside me stiffly. Rigid as a statue. Holding the gun in both hands and a finger on the trigger.

A blue ray projected out and formed a figure. It was my dad wearing bulky armor! The colors were identical behind the blue beam. He was in a different armor and not the one he wore before.

"Hello, Crasto."

"Who's Crasto?"

"You. My son."

"My name's Aaron! And I am not our son." I yelled.

"Oh, I assume why not?"

"I heard you talking to kill me that night on the phone with someone, and that's not what a father would do to his son!" I yelled again.

He chuckled.

"You're one sneaking bastard!" He said, shaking his head. "Now give me that freaking stone."

"What stone? I have been locked up in here for an eternity or so. How would I get a stone?"

"Don't you talk to me with that tone, alright? And the stone that a big man gave you while *he* was, I mean, I was away!"

"How do you know about that stone?"

"This isn't a school, kid! Enough questions. I need you to tell me where that stone is?"

"And you'll let me go?"

"No, I will not."

"Then, good luck with your quest!"

"Nobody tells me NO! I am asking you very delightfully, tell me where's the stone or get electrocuted, tell me?"

The guard behind me took his gun and turned in all the power to full. He pointed it at my neck and urged me to tell where it was.

He was clenching his teeth and sounded holding up anger.

"I would rather not."

"I've been asking you very politely, but you left me no choice. You forced me to use the harsh way. Go for it general." He darted his eyes to the guard, the general.

I looked at him. He nodded and cocked the gun.

As he turned to me, I pushed myself to run without a second thought. Feeling tremendous pain in my feet, I ran for my life, knowing that I would never get this chance again, so I used it.

The two were busy talking, and a few steps away from the exit, the dad shouted.

"Stop!"

Before anyone could come to their senses, I pressed 'CLOSE' on the keypad sprinting out of the cabin, and the door slid back closed.

They thumped the door badly. Vibrations could be felt from my feet up to my body. The further I ran, the lower the vibrations I felt. And suddenly, it stopped. And a loud swish was heard in the direction of the door.

They must've opened it. I sprinted faster, and the pain somehow began to fade away. I looked down. The gaps between my toes hinted at blood. I stopped. Looked at either side of both my feet. They were covered in blood. The cuts have oozed. They must've gone numb. I looked back. The blooded footprints called for my death. I could hear their footsteps approaching.

I took off my T-shirt and tore it in half. I tied both pieces on either foot.

I took the next right and then left, wondering where I was going, and the soldiers might be coming or were already on their way, and I may end up coming just before them. I was scared.

When I was at a reasonable distance from the door. I decided to rest for a few minutes, and I am sure they will be here soon. I found a gap behind two large pipes with absolutely no way to peek through. There was a small opening beneath the lower pipe, and I hoped to fit through it. I put my head into the gap and pushed myself in. I had trouble fitting my waist through it, so I pushed my pants down to my knees and pulled my body in, but my pants fell off the floor. I made my leg out, and I struggled to pull my pants in through a small opening between two pipes. Hopefully, I found a belt loop. I clutched it between my toe fingers and pulled it in. I grabbed the pant and held them near my chest. It was blistering in here, and I was already lying naked, sweating to hell. I was thirsty and wanted water. I peeked out and tried reading the labels laminated by glass shields beside the door in front of me.

It was some hell of a language. The words were unreadable, and some wrong scripts were written on them even if I was unfamiliar with the language.

My neck itched abruptly. The water leaking out in sweat may have caused it. I scratched the back of my neck and wiped the sweat off it. The words then were readable in a trice. I blinked once or twice to figure out what happened, actually! I was moving my hands all over the body, still watching out. And in a flash, I cannot reread those. That was highly prompted. I checked my hand on the back of my neck. I didn't know I had superpowers.

I shifted my hand from the back of my neck again, and it worked!

The label says-

SURVEILLANCE ROOM

I didn't know what surveillance meant as I had no dictionary. It was in my bag, but that's lost somewhere. Maybe here. I was melting down in there and was dying of dehydration. I had to figure something out.

There were no rooms around at my sight through the gap. There was also no one around in my sight. This door was my only hope and was worth taking the risk as the name's pretty captivated. I carefully pushed my leg out and pushed myself out. I warily walked to the door holding my pants in one hand, terrified of being caught. The door was enclosed with an advanced level of security. It asks for a seven-spaced password or an electronic authorization device!

I looked around. There was another room about fifty feet away. I walked to it. It required the same *bullshit!* I walked down to the third one about another two feet apart. They all mandated passwords above a silly keyboard displayed below it. The keyboard exhibited strange keys upon it with literally nothing encoded on it. Just keys.

I heard footsteps approaching this away. I let myself hide behind the wall and then entered a passway. I could listen to multiple footsteps approaching. I ran between the walls leading to alternate scenarios. Crossways leading to different quarters. I ran across every path I found relevant. A soldier abruptly appeared from the far left and pointed his gun at me, asking me to go on my knees while moving steadily.

He consciously leaves the gun in his left hand, holding it in either hand and bringing it near his mouth.

"I have found the kid!" He says with relief, still darting his eyes at me.

"Where?" A voice cracks through the transmitter.

"In Section 24-A, near the cockpit."

"Copy that. Coming in."

He loses his right hand, points the gun away, and sprints to me. I ran to the right in my defense. It must've loosened up some pounds today, I hope!

Someone pounced on me from the right. I struggled not to get seized by them. I heard them hushing me to not make noise. I opened my eyes, and it was her. The one with the gluey limbs.

"Wh- what are you doing?" I asked quietly, terrified and relieved simultaneously, trying to figure out what was happening.

"I'll explain it to you later. First, you have to find her."

"Find who?"

"Your Mo-" She paused. Looking away, she said, "The one who was with you in the apartment. Find her. She will tell you what you have to do."

"Why? What is happening? Who is she?"

"I am not authorized to tell you all this, but I am sure she is."

"Why? Where can I find her?" Still trying to understand a word she is talking about. "My life is in danger right now. What should I do?"

"Don't worry. He will help take you to her. You are our only hope!"

"Wait, wh-"

The soldier comes in, breaking through the liquid barrier.

"Time to go. They'll be here any minute now."

She gets up, and her limb pulls me up too.

"Apply this to wounds." She secreted the substance from her limbs and applied it to my toes and arms. "This will help. It acts as a healing factor and will help you recover."

He pulled me out of the barrier and rushed me back to where I hid.

"Hey, can you tell me what's going on?" I rebelled against him and pulled out my hand out of his grasp.

He looked around and unlocked the door. The door slid open. There were two people inside whom he shot dead before they could take any action.

I still looked in awe and the way he just ignored me. He asked me to get in.

"I will not! Until you tell me what is going on?"

"Okay then, die out there."

He had such a deep voice.

"They must be coming in any moment now." He said like he didn't care. "The only person you are safe with right now is me. So, get your ass in now."

He was right. He won. I got in embarrassed. The door slid back closed. Blood spattered encircled the place. The walls were sprayed with blood. The floor abounded with blood spreading across. I watched my step and tried to reach the chair. But eventually, had to step on the blood to get it. The room had a massive screen displaying different live footage from the cameras.

I saw different people walking and marching through the places holding guns in armor.

"Okay, so," he said. "You're the one."

"The one who?"

"The one who will save us from the massive extinction and stuff from the *Salkoprites*."

"I'm Aaron, and wait! Who are you first? And what extinction? What's Salkoprite?"

"You have no idea what I am talking about, huh?"

"Yes, until you tell me what the hell is going on!" I said, trying hard not to clench my jaw.

"You can call me Arleigh."

I took a deep breath. I wiped my damp eyes and said softly, "I don't know what's going on or whatever the hell the *saltoprites* are! I need to know. I was living a happy life, and then I don't know what happened to me that I decided to leave-"

I broke down.

I felt a hand on my back, "It's not your fault. It never was."

"Yes, it is! I shouldn't have left my house, then this would've never happened to me." I sobbed.

"What you did was correct. It was meant to be this way. Or in that scenario, you would've been killed by your father."

I felt the hand move away. He walked to another chair and sat opposite me.

"I'm sorry, kid! I am not authorized to tell you all this, but I can tell you just one thing."

"What?" I gazed up at him with hope.

"Years back, about millions of light-years away from K-10, there's XO142 at the outer edge of a galaxy what we call Messier 31. XO142 is approximately double the earth's size and mass. The planet was quite happy and satisfied with its needs. Has a Type I civilization and two moons – Gah and Beka and is currently working on building an artificial moon. Its population is approximate to the earth. There are eleven huge landmasses, and each landmass has a total of forty-five nations, each being ruled by a single king. The rest is covered with a shallow layer of water about a hundred meters in depth. You can call XO142 a destined planet. Whoever born there is being destined to do something. Each king to a farmer, even a foe to a best friend, everything is destined. You can't tell where your destiny is waiting, but you'll reach it. Depending on your faith and loyalty towards it, you can either reach your destiny in your sixties or even in your twenties. After every decade, ten warriors are born in each nation, destined to kill the nation's king and be the king. From childhood, they are trained. When the trainer announces they are ready, the warriors and the king fight. All ten versus one. Whoever kills the king gets the throne."

He said it all in one go.

"But the lady she talked about surely lies with the answer to your every question. We need to find her!"

"Wait! I have listened to this before!"

"From whom?" He got charged and alerted.

"From that woman here in prison. She told me the exact same thing in her apartment."

"I guess that's alright. You knew something beforehand."

"No, I mean the exact same thing! From all the vowels to your tone, exactly the same."

"Yes, we describe this the same because-"

"Because?"

"I am not getting it," he appeared confused and stressed.

"You'll get it. Let's find her first. We'll get to this later with her."

He got up from the chair and looked across the screen, hoping to find her. He went through every single footage of a total of one hundred twenty cameras.

Found her!

In our visual, she's in her cell two stories below the ground, guarded by six guards.

Another visual on the screen shows several guards marching toward us.

"They found us!"

He handed me a Glock from the holster around his waist.

Listen carefully, "No matter what, I have to get you out of here alive. Now, we don't have enough backup to fight all of them and reach her. You have to get out safely first. We can build up a plan later to save her. You understand?"

"But-"

A massive shatter detonated the whole area! The screens went black for a second, and the entire room trembled. He covered me immediately with his body. He then rose from the ground and checked the screens.

Someone just broke into the ship!

Chapter 11

Shootings were heard, screams too. And a lot of shouting. He opened the door and ordered me to follow him, which was quite an option, but I knew who was coming. I asked him to wait. They will be here.

"You know who are they?"

I was rather busy looking upon the surveillance area where most of the cams were back after the explosion searching for them.

"It's our chance to get her! Come on, now!" He said, loading up his gun.

"What happened?"

He spread his arms and said, "Change of plan!"

I hurried out and followed him with the Glock steady in my hand.

"If you see anyone, aim for the leg. That's their weak spot, understand?"

"Yeah!" I said, speeding.

He took a left, shooting two on the leg. Then right, killing four with his grenade. All the way front, throwing a stun grenade and escaping, then to the right, taking cover.

We were close to her. Security was increasing with every move. I was left with only two shells. Two shots, and I'm out!

I looked at him, signaling about the ammunition. He signaled back, saying he also had two grenades left. We needed to choose our shots wisely.

He signaled back again, saying she was just behind the next door.

"How do you know?" I signaled.

"Surveillance room."

He threw one grenade at the soldiers and a counter grenade at us made us stun after a failed try of retracting from it. That's when he threw his final grenade back at them, which was more of a smoky one. We tried to escape, but the indecisive firing was far from being over, and we had no choice but to take cover behind the walls. When they ceased their fire, it was a chance to get out and escape, but it was not until we realized we were surrounded by an army of soldiers.

That's when I heard you all.

Muffled noises were coming from a distance but were obscured by the blood pounding in my ears.

"Get the kid!" Someone shouted, now shooting nonstop at the soldier's legs.

It was Ryker!

My heart filled with hope. The hope I never saw coming. Just after Chloe and Mocker shot at them, all guns turned to them, and we escaped hiding behind the walls taking cover, gasping. I still had two shells left and handed over the Glock to him. He grabbed it and held my hand as we dashed to the next room.

Explosions and blasts were heard every other second. He shot the last two shots. One at the authorization screen and the other between the small void of the closed door. The space got bigger. Then he took out the snake camera from one of his side pockets. He inserted it in and turned it on. The screen appeared on the device on his forearm and examined the area.

He kicked the door and cussed. He said tiresomely, "She's gone! They took her."

"Took her? But where?" I said instantly, looking at him with awe. Not knowing what to do next.

"I don't know! I told them it was not a good idea." He sighed.

He took out the snake camera and put it back in his pocket.

"We need to get away from here now." He roared, getting furious.

So suddenly, a car drove frantically past us. Skidding as they drifted and turned to us. The screeching of the tires was hitting me and left its marks on the floor. The car door opened while in motion, and Chloe asked to get in. The car was in no condition. The bullet marks covered the entire vehicle, with windows cracked with bullet shots. The front windows had no mirrors, and the windshield was cracked up.

We got in the car. Ryker was driving while Carlos was up in the front seat, and Chloe was in the back seat. She loaded her rifle and shot, peeking out the window.

"Go, Go, Go!" Carlos shouted while shooting the soldiers coming in from behind. Ryker revved the engine.

He pressed and swiped some fingers on the screen, and the marble-shaped ball attached to the car's trunk emitted a blueish ray up around the vehicle and created a shield while the soldiers shot, and suddenly the bullets couldn't penetrate the shield. Ryker examined the whole process and then swiped another few fingers on the screen, and I could feel his fingers trembling and sweat glimmering from his hand. He paused and looked at everyone, and swiped his finger. The car shook and elevated. I would say it was floating in the air. "Buckle up!" Ryker said, holding on to the steering and Carlos leaning on his seat, constructing a grip with his legs and arms behind Ryker's seat.

"Wait, how do you have this tech?" He said in disbelief and adjusted his seating position to a little more to Ryker.

"What do you mean?" Chloe asked, adjusting her position to Arleigh.

Arleigh changed his position to Chloe and said in a confusing yet frightening voice, "How did you get this tech? This belongs to the Xalkrea's."

There was a wave of silence in the car.

"Xalkrea?"

"I can't tell you much, but we will have a long discussion on this, and you're gonna tell me where is the ship?"

Chloe asked me to hold her hands. I held her hand with my left and his hand with my right, but he grasped me by my waist to ensure my safety. I looked back through the rear windshield. They had seized their fire and stared at us, levitating up.

"What is happening?"

"We're jumping! Don't you wanna get out of here?"

A substantial rumbling noise starts to build. About every part of the car-cum-aeroplane shakes terribly. I looked at Ryker. He was looking a bit confused, and seeing Carlos this quiet gave me the chills of the forthcoming storm.

"What's wrong?" Asks Carlos.

"I don't know," his hands now trembling more than ever. Looking at what's wrong.

"Do it! I don't wanna die too for this piece of shit!"

He took out a gun and pointed at my head, ready to pull the trigger, but Arleigh, from the other end, tossed the gun from his hand and chopped his wrist bone with a blow without much effort.

He cried in pain! Blood spluttered out his palmless limb. His palm fell at the bottom of the car.

Chloe watched in disbelief. She felt disgusted. I could clearly say that with the expression on her face. Carlos groaned and cried inconsolably in the front seat. That was the first time I had felt bad for him.

Chloe verbally burst open at Arleigh. On the other hand, he didn't care and wiped his glove, which indeed had a knife thing in it and could tear up possibly everything. But when I questioned him, all he had in his defense was that *he did it to protect me from him. It's what he's assigned, and he will even make drastic decisions if he had to for my safety.* It was heartwarming, but not the right time to acknowledge it.

The shield had started to disintegrate as the soldiers opened their fire indiscriminately upon us. Impacts could be felt by us while the car shuddered and thundered tremendously.

"What is wrong, Ryker? You need to get us out now!" Chloe seemed tensed and panicking.

"I'm trying this ain't working now. It has worked forever, but why not now?"

A shot hit the car's trunk through the disintegrating shield.

All systems went black for a second, and loud shouting came from Chloe's end.

"RYKER?"

The systems went off. The car crashed to the ground and fractured into pieces. I was clasped onto Arleigh. He pushed me aside and kicked off the car door. He emerged pissed. He grabbed his guns and charged at the soldiers unaided. Nobody shot at him but threw an electric net at him to which he zapped and passed out.

In time, all soldiers stood at attention and cleared the way in the middle. It was so silent in there now. We can hear the footsteps approaching. Let me tell you, listening to those was horrifying. Chloe looked up at Ryker and tried to wake him up. He was too passed out. Carlos was trying hard to hold on to his screams. Chloe was loading her guns.

"Well, well, well… Who do we have here?"

The voice is recognizable.

"Why are y'all trying so hard to save him? I don't understand. He gets in trouble, and you come to save him, and now you're in trouble too. Tough luck! Tch! Tch!"

I know who it is. It's my father.

"And. It's for my son if he can hear. It's all a lie. A goddamn lie!" His voice sharpened. "Bring them in."

They threw a ball, liberating a gas with a soft explosion. Chloe shot a few times at it, but the bullets diverged. A shot bounced at it and hit Carlos in the leg. Carlos was already passed out due to the gas. Luckily we didn't hear his scream this time.

Hinged onto a handcuff. Kneeled on both knees. Sweat trickled down my face. I looked up. My body asks for forgiveness at every movement. We were again where this chase began - the cabin.

Dad sat in a hovering egg chair with glowing silent geometrical thrusters. 'The two' now stood against the door guarding it. I could sense the rage in their thickened black eyes. Four body-suited soldiers stood parallel to each other, encircling me with their chin up, chest out, shoulders back, and stomach in. Arms fixed at the side, thumb at the grip, and index finger at the trigger of the guns in their arms.

"Wh... What do you," I asked weakly. "What do you want from me?"

"Kid," he said, softening his voice. "See, I know you don't trust me anymore right now, but if there's even the slightest chance for you to give me a chance to explain, I'll be-"

"DO YOU REALLY THINK I'M AN IDIOT?" That rage just escaped through my mouth.

He gave a most disappointing but understandable reaction.

"Okay," he said softly, "Just remember whatever they said you are nothing but a mere lie."

"What do you mean?" I scoffed with my most disapproving face. "Where are they, huh? Arleigh and the ones in that car?"

"Oh, they. Yes," he clicked his tongue and acted if as he don't remember. "They're fine. Maybe dead. Maybe behind the ward. Who cares?"

"I care. They were here to save me. They have a reason for risking their lives to get me out of here, not like you who wants me dead."

He slighted a smirk like he was expecting this answer.

He stood up, and his egg chair transfigured into a staff that skimmed right into his hand.

"If I wanted you dead, you won't be answering that question," he stated with his eyebrows raised as if making an argument. "Do you wanna meet her?" His voice deepened.

Some portion of the wall slid back with a rough mechanical sound and spun upwards. A faint figure in a metal wheelchair with light green linings glided towards him. It was more of a hover-chair. The portion behind swiveled back to the wall. It was her. The one from the apartment. She looked exhausted, but it appeared that the chair was healing her. It had a monitor which displayed her vitals and her healing percentage. I could not properly see, but I speculated it as twenty.

"Yeah, there you are!" He bestowed a villainous smile. "Aren't you gonna tell him the truth?" His voice echoed across the cabin.

"Leave…" she struggled, "leave him… ALONE!"

She put her all in that one and fell on the backrest of the chair.

"Oh, I don't think I will."

He banged the staff on the ground with a loud thud! The dark glassed elongated sphere upon the staff radiated a bright blue glare of light, and the whole cabin was remodeled into this empty space with distant stars twinkling, burning up their fuels. A voice from him continued.

"Long ago, while your solar system was still phasing of fast-stirring dust and clouds, there was a planet far away millions of light-years away where life was just in its phase."

The hologram projectors projected an Earth-like planet that zoomed in to satisfy eyes with its beautiful yet strange creatures walking and sprinting in hordes over a grassy landscape, roaring and muffling in their plays. A small horde of baby creatures dashed toward a mid-sized creature. They were cute in appearance - What the Hell? - They jumped and attacked that one-eyed animal biting and scribbling off bits of its skin and eventually gouging its eye out. The animal screeched and shrieked to death.

"The evolution on Earth was unexplainably similar to what took place here," He breathed and waved his hand. The scene time lapsed to a building-sized asteroid striking planet in its deep oceans. The winds ran off, causing massive high-altitude waves and tsunamis throughout the globe. It turned into a ball of fire, ejecting out debris from the impact. The debris clustered and collided over and formed a satellite to the planet. Though this lasted only a minute in the lapse - he now paused it somewhere.

"Wait, what's that?" I gasped.

"Those are the Eliopsdki's," a huge spacecraft with small glimmering windows. It was like a building flowing in this anti-gravity with thrusters on its ends and base. Accompanied by a huge oval-like tank fixed on its top. "They were and still are the most advanced species in the galaxy. They go take on different planets but only those which are vacant or were wiped out, by any means. They must've seen this on their radars or must've been reported by their emissaries."

"That doesn't make any sense!" I scoffed.

"Wanna meet one of them?" He yet again delivered a villainous smile, this time with a slight laugh. "Bring him in!"

The wall swiveled back, revealing a figure trapped behind a hexagonal sphere on a trolly, and walking with him were three guards. One pushing the trolly and two guarding. They parked and kicked the sphere beside Dad, and walked away. The wall spun back and closed the entrance. The Eliopsdkian grunted. It was blue-faced with a yellow-blue body down the neck. It had metalized stripes on its forehead running down to the back of its neck. It seemed vengeful. Its two-eyed face said it all. A face similar to humans.

"I assume you have the stone." It said.

"I haven't seen you in long. How are you?" Dad laughed. "And FYI, I don't, but I have its keeper and someone you may know.

It turned and scrutinized me with its eyes. Its face rose to disbelief.

"Is it really-?" It gasped, and tears trickled down his eyes to chin, turning the skin yellow.

"Oh yes, it is." Dad clicked his tongue.

The Eliopsdkian turned violent and started kicking the sphere.

Dad laughed at it and stated that it was unbreakable and that he was just wasting his energy.

He continued punching and kicking the sphere. I could literally see the anger and helplessness in his moves. And there it was, a crack in the sphere. Those bleeding knuckles proved his strength.

Dad's flabbergasted face said it all.

"Woah!" He raised his eyebrows, "I think I underestimated you. Put him in another stronger case with a gas mask on. Block the airpipe and make him *suffocate!*"

The guards beamed out a gravity-defying wave through their guns. The sphere elevated, and they threw it on the trolly. The Eliopsdkian grunted badly.

"I am gonna get you out!" He said in a low agonizing voice, his hands pressed against the sphere.

The guard pulled the trolly as the wall swiveled back and then back again.

Dad clicked his tongue as he watched him go. There was a sense of freakiness in his looks.

"Okay, so… uhh...," he blanked. "Yes, where were we?"

"Who was he and how does he know me?"

"Who doesn't," he chuckled. "He was the senior executive commander of the Eliopsdkian forces."

"So how did you get him?"

"It's a long story kid, we ain't have time for that, it's just that we lost our best forces to catch him."

He clicked his tongue.

"Commander, you need to focus," A soldier standing near the controller said.

He nodded and swung his staff to now project the Eliopsdkian ship landing onto that planet and revealing themselves as masked with similar linings on their forehead. One of them ordered to bring dozens of capsules and then unlatched them on the surface.

"The only purpose of the Eliopsdkian species is to reanimate life on these abandoned planets with their experimental species they create by merging the DNA of species around the world and sometimes the galaxy and then abandoning them here. It's how they work! Unless here, this demonstration here created something bigger than them. They never in their life had dreamt of."

The animals were latched onto some tubes, which were yanked off as they tried to stand. A six-legged animal jumped off from the hatched capsule with a crazy blood-stricken mind and started slaughtering other species as it chomped and squelched on their bodies.

"What's happening?" I asked, frightened and confused.

"That is the law of nature. Killing off the weaker ones. Stronger overpowers the weaker."

"That's so wrong," a body from the other egg moved and squelched as its parts readjusted themselves, forming a structure similar to a child in the mother's womb. "Now, what the hell is that?"

"They are forming themselves. One of the most unique and beautiful evolutions in the whole of the universe," the body formed itself and stood with its five, six, seven- ***eight*** eyes closed on its two human-like legs! The structure of the body was similar to humans. Tall. Muscular. "Now watch!"

The 6-legged animal that stood near the mangled bodies of the weak, sensed and dashed berserk at him. He stood still. As it approached him, he jumped in the air and landed with his kick on its back and held his neck with a twist. It yelped its last cry.

The Eliopsdkians celebrated his extraordinary flexes.

It turned to them and approached them. The guards behind activated and pointed their weapons at it.

He stopped about 5 feet from her – The figurehead, and kneeled.

"My lord, you created me. You are and will be revered by me. Give me a purpose for what you've created me. How may I serve you?" It spoke with a low and respectful tone.

"You are one of our experiments. To repopulate this world that has been left abandoned in the past. You don't clearly have a purpose."

"You saw what happened and what I am capable of, I cannot live off alone with these stupid pungent animals. I need a purpose, my majesty!"

"You need a purpose?" she said. "You'll have to earn it. Find and build your own. A few people get those odds.

"But my majesty, how?"

"That's why we created you. Your life won't have left any meaning if it were to be known by us or you or anyone."

She turned and hovered off into the quin jet. The guards marched into another jet. They blew off into a spaceship in orbit.

"It was the best they created." Dad clicked his tongue.

The presentation paused.

"What happened?" I asked, jumbled about his intention of the click.

"They underestimated him. By a lot. He did everything to find his purpose. Once he traveled all of the woods on the planet, swam through the oceans to find that he was immortal. He cannot be wasted to death by natural forces or become a saggy old doddering whack. He traveled every corner of his world and found nothing. He tried to talk, but everyone feared him. He chopped down the trees, built a house, but never lived in it. The restlessness won't let him sleep. Sometimes he went to fight the creatures in the waters. They were not his competitors. He passed his life but never lived it. Things changed later on. Other experimental life-forms began to die due to changing atmospheres but he remained all alone bearing the pain of his existence."

"Did they return?"

"Yes, they did, and it was only for the unfortunate."

"What happened?"

"They returned after centuries to look back at the process and developments. However, for them, it was almost a decade in which they found everything dead on their return. The only mortal area they found was a shack at the center with a radius of flowers. While they investigated the site, he tried to sneak into their jets. But an alert was sent to the guards as he did not match their body scan."

"Then?" I don't know why I worried, but it sounded concerning.

"He gave himself in, never trying to resist their force, bent to his knees, and asked forgiveness. Their majesty came in giving him another chance for his obscenity and expressed her appreciation for his patience and diligence towards her. She awarded him his purpose. What he longed for. The only purpose she said was to serve her and be her another pathetic slave just like they had been doing for years. He was never more disappointed in his life and for the first time in his centuries of years had torn his eyes. It was agony, the pain, to wait for something your whole life and get nothing. He dashed to the soldiers and tore all of them apart as they open fire on him. The majesty while in midst of this violence stood and grabbed him by his neck to pass him out as he went for her."

"She sounds stronger than I thought."

"She's way more than you think, yes," he said, sitting back on the chair as the staff disintegrated and the projection wobbled away. "They then took him with them."

–

Alert buzzed in the cabin. Dad stood from the chair with his staff stick.

"What's happening?" Dad shouted. "What are they?"

I was frightened. I tried to stand for an escape. He clasped me by the neck and squeezed it into a suffocating panic.

"Stay there!" He threw me back to the ground. "You've got some guts, kid."

I gasped for my breath. Rolled onto the ground, hyperventilating, and then coughed violently. A spoonful of blood coughed out of my mouth and stained the metal floor. My eyes watering spontaneous tears of pain, remorse, and identity crisis – Mostly pain.

A regiment dashed in through the door. They looked antsy.

"What are they?" He asked, walking whilst shaking progressively. With every foot he took, he sounded deeper until he stood face-to-face with the leader – the colonel.

"It's the Eliospdkians," He said with a dreadful voice. "They broke into Roche limit this very minute. It's confirmed they sent in two of their force units. They'll be here any minute, sir!"

Sweat broke down his face. He seemed daunted and overstrung by all the lies he splashed into my face, would burst out free, and this aviary would burn to the ground of his fabricated flex about his alliance.

I looked at him just the way he gazed at me with a slight tensed head shake – a cat on a hot tin roof.

A shock wave detonated the whole area.

Chapter 12

Dad swung his staff as he jumped on me. The staff liquidated into a dome-shaped barrier with absolute darkness. He clapped, and the dome transparentized to see the chaos emerge through the flickering of the lights. The roof was blown away into pieces, and mud dripped onto the floor. The systems were down. The only light on the opposite side of the impact flickered.

His face paled after he watched some of his guards slaughtered amidst the invasion he never suspected.

"How the hell did they find out about this place?" He exclaimed. The smoke curled as the fried systems exploded into tiny explosions. "It is not possible!"

I approached the barrier, faced my palm onto it, and eyed for the two and one who always electrocuted me. The smoke after the explosion was so dense that everything seemed to be engulfed within its thickness. As the smoke blew upward, the thickness diluted. I couldn't spot them.

"Let's go!" He said.

"But my shackles?"

He popped out the top plate of his right forearm and stretched his arm. The band on his wrist turned green, and the dome disintegrated into the staff and swifted into his hand. The band turned red. He swung his staff again. The band was now colored blue, and the staff turned into a green holographic blade. The band turned green. He sliced the shackle chain in half.

I helped myself up. The smoke suffocated the rubbled area. I coughed after I inhaled some of it.

Dad noticed me coughing violently. He reached out for an oxygen mask and placed it on my mouth. The mask's ends elongated and vacuumed to my mouth.

"Here, Breathe! One breath at a time."

I inhaled harshly. After a few deep breaths, I can feel the oxygen running.

The soil stopped dripping down. The bright ray of light shone through the hole onto the mounted soil. The sunlight filtered the dust as it brightened the room.

I can now spot the guards helping one another up behind the smoke. I ran my eyes. I saw the general lying dead beneath the debris that fell on him. Wait, he's not! He moved and pushed the rubble away with his hands, his armor damaged, on the guard lay dead behind him. I looked at the other sides.

Near the gate, one of the two lay dead with a huge splinter in his head. The other sat beside him, holding his hand, and shrieked tears of agony.

"We need to go, come on!" Dad said.

He pulled my hand hard, which I resisted and tried to push him away. He squeezed his hand hard, though, that I felt a crack in my arm. It was not painful. It was not the bone. It was the snap, just like from knuckles.

"Come with me I said!" Dad warned sternly as he clenched his teeth.

He pulled me to the gateway, which malfunctioned after the blast and was stuck half open. I passed past one of the two, who shrieked and held the other in his arms. Dad approached him and said we don't have time for this; There's a bigger problem we're dealing with. It's not your fault, Seltul. We'll have their funeral – if we survive. He stood up and wiped his tears, and appeared belligerent.

Dad grabbed me by his other hand and initialized another holographic sword from his suit's forearm. He sliced away the gate and pushed me through it. Dad walked in and followed him was red-eyed, revengeful Seltul.

"Call in the soldiers!" Dad said. The general, too, followed us after he noticed us exiting the area. We walked through the malfunctioned quarters with blinking lights and dangling wires from the ceiling.

"On it sir," said the General. He sterned his voice and swiped fingers on the broken screen of his forearm suit. "Soldiers, gear in for the battle. They are Eliospdkians. Yes, they are alive. They have crossed the Roche limit and know where we are. We need to be careful. They'll be here any minute. Put on your suits, cover the entries, and brace your hearts – This is going to be a bloodbath."

His speech was motivating and concerning as I was not with them!

"Get me updates on intruders, Seltul," Dad said.

He nodded and turned right on the next split.

"Where are we going?" I asked.

"To my quarter," he said. "I have my weaponry and suits there."

"Where's Arleigh?"

He brisked towards his quarter down the hallway and was stopped by the dysfunctioned elevator, broken by the sudden impact.

He stood in repose for a few seconds.

We heard shootings far away up the hallway and explosions as the lights flickered. He suddenly activated his blade and sliced away the metal from the automatic doors of the elevator. The general pushed me into the elevator. Dad cut away the elevator floor to reveal the unending dark fall. They, both, activated the flashlights on their suits, and Dad removed my oxygen mask. Dad deactivated his blade as he looked down the hole, counting away floors to his quarter.

I gasped for breath for a second. It felt weird. I coughed. Dad disintegrated his staff into some magnetic hand grips and broke them into two. He gave them to me. They were two square-like structures with flat surfaces and enough space to hang both hands on.

"We are going down," Dad said. "Follow me and don't try anything funny."

Dad activated magnetic thrusters on his suit and banged into the walls.

"Come in," he said.

I stood near the hole as I looked deep within the menacing endless. I slowly put my legs in the hole after I sat on the edge. Dad pushed himself below after he grunted to move his hand down.

I pondered the idea of renouncing the thought of going down.

"I am not going," I said. I felt a sudden frustrating push from the back. "Ahh, what the fwah-"

The hand grips were stuck to the wall. I hung above the death hole, and by this point, it sounded sweet. My heart pounded out of my mouth and barely swooshed a sound.

I looked up. It was the General who pushed me. I looked down. Dad was already pushing himself down. I tried moving down. I pulled my left hand away and placed it down to my chest. I then placed my right hand near my face. By this, my hands were already strained and wanted rest. I looked down for motivation.

I closed my eyes and breathed a heavy sigh. I pulled both my hands to my chest again, one after another. I looked down at Dad. He slid down the surface and suddenly tapped on his forearm screen. He stopped. A spark charged out as he halted with a screech. He altered the strength of the magnets enough to slide him down. I thought I could do that as well. I scrutinized my handgrips and found nothing.

Then, by no means I suddenly slid down, screaming as I could not control the speed. It halted, my grip slipped out of my fingers, and I fell into the darkness. My heart skipped beats, for I was too stunned to scream. I felt a hand on my collar after I passed through a light from the wall. I encountered a sharp pain in my throat. My T-shirt noosed me for a split second. It was my Dad; he had reached his quarter. I smiled. He threw me in.

I grunted. I coughed and pulled down my T-shirt. I felt my neck. It was itchy and red as I looked at the mirror before me on the wall. Wait, the entire wall was the mirror. I was almost a victim of strangulation by a T-shirt - how embarrassing! I gazed across the quarter, coughing and swallowing in on coughs. A white marble-like round table was kept before a fluffy black sofa. Dad walked down to the mirror, swiveled his hands, and rippled the screen as he pushed his hands into the mirror to his elbow. He clocked his hands to the right. As such, he was rotating something within. He pulled back his arms with the push to the screen in opposite directions as if revealing something. His hands were not wet. The screen rippled and waved away to the ground into a few discs placed uniformly, displaying his arsenal. Racks of gun blasters arranged to the right, and armor and vests stacked on the wall. Grenades and hand-equipments positioned uniformly at the center. He disassembled his suit.

"Why? Why did you do this Dad?" I asked, begging, hoping to get a reason.

He sighed. He looked for a new one in the stacks and chose one. It was the coolest one. It was in parts. He placed the forearm piece, and it extended and covered his entire arm. Then, he set another piece on his other arm. He placed the chest piece, and it grew to the back and locked flawlessly to its arm pieces. He put on the leg pieces, and they extended and locked to his arm body.

"Dad?" I cried. "Say something!"

With headgear in his hands, he espied me and sighed. "You still have no idea," he smirked. "Really, I mean how can you be so stupid, Aaron?"

"You need to tell me," I said. "That stone. What is with that stone? I don't have it. You have everything I own. Just let me go. I'll never tell anyone about you."

"I know you don't have it, but still I can't let you go."

"You do? Then why are being such an ass? Just let me go!"

"Where did you learn that language from?" He was surprised. "It doesn't matter if you have it. It has you."

"It has me? What do you mean?"

"It was designed by your real father for you," he said, emphasizing. "It's attached to you like a parasite but not as a host. It instead nurtures you. It has a consciousness of its own. It follows you, no one knows how but it does. It's something out of this world that he designed for you, and the key to get to it is you. It knows you're here with us, and it'll do something to save you."

"My father?" My mind rose. Listening to that somehow sparked courage and confidence in me that I had a paucity of. "You knew him?

"Not personally, but yes." He said. "One of the best intellects and warriors of this galaxy.

"Who is he?"

He smiled, almost chuckled. "Xalk, the one created by Eliospdkians, who ruled this very galaxy for over a thousand years."

My mind blew away. "The one you told me about a few hours ago?"

"Yes that one," he said, putting on his headgear which locked with a click and the entire suit integrated into one. "Certainly a once in an eternal mind, but not a great warrior with the whole universe in context."

He looked menacing and belligerent. That suit activated, and its eyes displayed a light green tint. He grabbed grenades and put them into the slots with popped out of the suit as he tapped on his chest. Took an entrenching gun and hung it around his arms.

I gulped on my dry mouth. "Where is he, my father," my voice intonated. My head felt lighter. My heart's ebullient. "Is he alive?"

"According to stories, he died a venerable death," he said. His voice solid. "You should be proud of him."

"But?"

A call distressed him. He swiped his finger on his arm. He stood in silence.

I was reminiscing and lost in the sketch of what my father would look like. The thought ran around, and my sight was blinded by my thoughts, "was he really the one he told me earlier in the control room? Am I... Am I not Hu... Human?! That makes no sense. He had such powers and I've none. Surely, this doesn't make any sense. He's lying."

"Seltul, get away from there!" He shouted. "Just get away. We're in –"

We heard screaming and shots above us. It was the General. He and Seltul fell down the shaft. Dad held on to his gun and grabbed me behind him.

"Stay there," he said.

I looked around hastily. There was a frame on either side. A chair around a desk stacked with several books and a picture of a woman. What caught my sight was a bag lying on the chair.

It's my bag! I crawled steadily to the desk behind me. Dad was locked in position to the shaft opening. I reached for the chair and pulled my bag down tactically. I hugged the bag and pushed my hand forward. I pulled my buttocks back to take the comfort of the wall. The bangings of the metal clanks faded away. He seemed confused. He pulled on his forearm, and his staff magneted back to him after it liquidated from the hand grips.

He grabbed the staff and flung it to display the footage of the above quarters. It disintegrated and projected the footage. The lift was gnarring blue. I remembered the shootings in her room. The soldiers who died spurred out blue. It's blood. I unzipped my bag to search for water if I had kept any. I found a bottle and shook it. It had plenty. I flipped the cap and gulped to its last drop. I wanted more. My lips dried out soon. Dad scrutinized the footage as he looked everywhere around the quarters.

"It's him," he said. He paused a frame. I peeked. It was the eliospdkian he showed me. He must've broke out of that sphere. "But how?"

Dad looked around aimlessly thinking.

"Fuck," he shouted. "The glass break leaked his information from the sphere."

"What," I questioned. "What are you talking about?"

"The sphere was built to hold his signals to prevent Eliospdkians to get his location. Now, since that was cracked, it must've leaked, inviting the Eliospdkians to my ship."

I scoffed, "Stupid."

"Did you say something?"

"No sir."

He skimmed through the footages constantly.

"They're retreating," he said. "We need to get out of here."

I looked around hopelessly.

He integrated his staff and reached out to me. He held my arm tightly and lifted me up. I grunted in pain.

"We need to hurry."

He sliced down the metal from the back wall. Exposing a cold dark entrance. He entered, and the area illuminated the lost hopes of Dad. The space jets and aviators were destroyed in the radiance of the walls.

"Fuck." He shivered and fell to the ground. "Fucking eliospdkians."

I looked around and chuckled. The broken ships burnt in fuel and destroyed fumed the eliospdkian dominance on his face. It was the hint of power they carried to destroy worlds amidst their creation of them. He brought his transmitter close to him.

"We're down, sire. I hope, in the time you receive this message, I'll be powdered to death and it's better than to face you. Kosta!"

"You shouldn't have messed with me, Dad."

"Messed," he chuckled. He unhooked his headgear and held it near his thighs. He looked at me and stood up to walk right into my face. "Everything that has happened is because of you."

He clenched his teeth as he shouted, spurting out saliva.

"I did not ask for any of this."

"Yes, it was my mistake that I agreed to adopt you."

"What do you mean?"

"Your father sent you to Earth to save you, but your ship crashed into nowhere. No one knows where, but you, you ended up with your mother. She was an ally of your father, a queen for her land, abandoned by her people. Only she knew your coordinates, so she sought a life with you here on this planet. I, on the other hand, had to get to you. I met her and set everything up just to get to you. We got married, and I eventually fell in love with her and the thing that bothered me was her affection to you that held me to this day. Until that day, while returning from the woods. The disappearance of that restaurant. I got the hint that it was them. The eliospdkians. Things began to get worse when she got the call. That's where everything broke. I was getting late for my job, and I realized it with those subtle hints that began growing explicit as time passed on. We made that call to lose her. She was a threat to our plan. But, she had already received her rejection for the job a week ago before that call. She got suspicious. She played the role. That night, she started the talk we hadn't had in years. She asked me everything so smartly that I couldn't answer her anymore. That's what I loved her for. I believe she knew what I was up to and she played her part to go away. Also, she wanted you to hear all of that. She instantly began shouting the stuff she wanted you to hear. Enough, to make you leave the house. Later that day when I went out, I met your mother. We talked, and she confronted everything she suspected about me. She showed me the stone. It's painful to reminisce but I defeated her, sent her here, and locked her in. During the battle, she threw her stone to her peer and he gave that to you."

"Fuck!" I held myself by the wall. I grabbed my head. It all made sense now. "It all makes sense now."

"You are dead either way, kid. He is going to kill you or the eliospdkians will."

"You need to tell me where everyone's locked up."

"Do I look like a slow-brainer to you?"

"No. Yeah. You are saying eliospdkians will kill me, right? Why would they kill me? I am the last of the Xalkrea."

"That's the reason."

"You're lying. They are no -"

An array of light shone through the roof, and a holographic figure appeared.

She was a woman with long grey hair and a thin suit. She gave relaxed and bold vibes that horrified me. Her face neutral. Her suit, thin as cloth, covered up to her neck and exposed skin through designs on her arms. Her legs covered with suit up to her toes. She wore no shoes – maybe her suit worked as shoes and provided padding.

"Crossa!" Dad revoked.

"Hello, darling! It's been time since I last saw you," she smiled and turned her face graciously to greet him. It appeared sarcastic. "How is your master serving you? A lot of pain, I believe, seeing your current position."

She chuckled.

"Serving him got me everything you never would've gotten me."

"I believe you."

He gave out an annoying grunt.

"Come on, kid," she turned to me. "You're the last Xalkrea and son of our creation?"

"I hope so. Everyone's telling me the same shit," I said. "It would be disheartening to hear he isn't now."

She smiled and then chuckled.

"Interesting. You got a sense of humor," she said, squinching her eyes at me. "He programmed you with all the deficiencies he had or that he disliked. He made you a better version of himself."

I raised my eyebrows for what she said.

"So, where's the stone," She asked.

"You won't have it," Dad said, looking into her eyes and standing up. "You bitch."

He spit.

She smiled.

"I don't have it," I said. "How do I assure you this?"

"It's always with you," she clenched her teeth which horrified the shit out of me. "Stop playing with me, kid. Every time we try to get to you, some of your people take you away from us."

"What do you mean?" Does that mean that trailer, the restaurant, all of that was you?"

"Yes."

"That recovery was not a dream?"

She seemed baffled. "Wha… What recovery?"

"After the trailer incident I almost died, I believe," I said. "I had some flashes and ended up on a bench near my house."

She took a little time to process. Then she looked straight at me.

"You need to come with me."

"No," Dad said. "He won't go anywhere with you."

She sighed and scratched her eyebrow.

Dad charged up his suit and put out a glowing, buzzing blade.

"You really wanna do this," she said.

"I do," Dad said. "Why don't you come in here, you coward bitch. So we can have a fair."

Suddenly the holographic lights retracted back and revealed her. Exactly the same, but then what she carried was a sword.

Dad dashed at her and sliced the air around her neck as she swung back. Dad found his balance about instantly. Dad went berserk and attacked her directly on her neck. She blocked it and stood still. She showed no work or sweat while Dad was sliding on his toes. Dad yelled at her face and slid his blade along hers, which sparked out and went for the legs. She jumped and stood still. He yet again went for her, and she shoved her sword in his gut through his back. He groaned. The sword pierced through the toughest suit he wore. She twisted it. He spurted out blood. She looked at him in the eye.

"You tried, Egtheran," she said. "But this story isn't yours to fight. It's mine."

She pulled out her sword, and blood flushed out like a fountain. He fell to the floor. He coughed and groaned. I stood there thinking about what to do. He wanted to kill me. She wanted to kill me. That alien wanted to kill me. I had no one to save me. Just surrounded by the people who wanted to cut me open. I am fucked, don't I?

"Now you," she said. "So, second thoughts on giving me the stone?"

"I don't have it," I said. "How many do I have to say?"

"You know what? That's it. I am gonna kill you and get that stone myself."

She proceeds toward me.

Dad chuckles. She stops and looks beside her. I look at him. He laughs.

"What's so funny?" She asked.

"You don't understand," he said. "This story ain't about you, bitch. This fucking story belongs to him, my son, and your doom, the Salkoprites. You. You are just a phase. Just as I was."

"I am no phase," she said. "The Salkoprites don't have anything to do with us."

"I know," Dad said. "They have to do with him."

She nods her head negatively. "I am ready to face them. They'll never know where he is. You don't have to worry."

"Aaron, your friends are in the prison cell. Go get them," Dad said. "Find your mother. She'll guide you."

"What the hell are you talking about," she laughed. "Do you really think he has a chance?

"Check your bag, son."

I unzipped my bag and put my hand in it. I went through the stuff. She looked at me with keen eyes. I felt something smooth, hard, and irregular.

"SHIT!"

She understood. She prepares to charge herself toward me. Dad charged his blade and sliced away one of her feet up the ankle. She crashed to the ground. Screaming of pain.

Dad stood up. "Hold it and think. Feel yourself close to them. Breathe -"

She swung her sword, and Dad's head flew out to the ground. His eyes stuck open, and his tongue lolled out. The eyes stared right through my soul.

"NO!" I screamed.

Blood spurted out to the ground, and his body crashed.

She struggled to stand up. She groaned.

"Give that to me," she said.

I closed my eyes. Tears cherished down. I walked upon my memories of them. Their faces. The woman from the apartment, Arleigh, Chloe, Ryker, and Carlos – the pain in the ass. I opened my eyes. She was about to throw her sword at me. I startled.

"Give me that -"

-

I stood in the hallway. Prison cages on either side. My heart's pounding through my head. I could feel my veins throbbing. My scalp itched due to sweat. Tears rushed down my cheeks. Dad. I can feel his blood on me. Mixed with mine on my T-shirt. Turned Purple. It stinks the same. I picked the unstained part of my cloth and wiped my face. It was red.

"Aaron."

A breaking female voice encountered beside me. I stood up and turned around into flickers of a light roof.

It was Chloe. She stood stunned and looked at me with hope. I brisked to her.

"Get us out of here, kid."

"Us?"

A figure arose out of the flickering to the jail barrier. It was Ryker.

"I am here too, shithead." The mocker walked out to the barrier.

"Great," I scoffed. "You survived?"

"Of course I did," he squinched his eyes.

I turned to see the opposite cell. It was dark. I walked closer and closer to the barrier. My face less than an inch away from it. A hundred sharp teethed mouths came out of the blue. I creamed back and fell to the floor. I almost had a cardiac arrest. It growled and roared at me through the barrier. It was kind of a huge piranha but on four legs and no tail. Carlos, on the other hand, burst out in laughter.

"Stupid kid," he said. "We came for him? I told ya it was a bad idea."

I forced myself up and walked to him.

"Listen you fuckhead! I never called you here. You came down here yourself. I thought it was nice of you that you came, but you seem to have come here to put me in more problem than I am already in and enjoy it to satisfy your soul. You think this all is funny? Wait, till you meet that lady. The Queen. She would snap you to dust. And she's coming here anytime now. What I want from you is to stop fucking yourself and help us get back up there. Do you understand?"

He appeared outraged. He punched the barrier and walked in. I looked at Ryker and Chloe. They looked at me with new eyes. It felt good.

"Aaron?" A voice encountered two cells ahead of this one. I ran to it. It was Arleigh.

"Are you okay?" Arleigh asked.

"Yes, I am," I said. "We need to get out of here. The Queen of Eliospdkians is here."

"Well, she'll help us. She's on our side."

"It didn't appear so," I scoffed. "She tried to kill me for that stone."

"What? Why?"

"I don't know. But she'll be here soon and we need to leave. She has killed my Dad."

"The head of Asarkians? No," he said. "Now, listen to me! There's a password to this cell. I'll tell it to you and just put that in, okay?

"Yeah, I can do that. What's that?"

"Okay, swipe three fingers down on this barrier.

I swiped three fingers down. Several things appeared on the screen.

"Can you read them?"

"No! Am I supposed to read them? They seem out of place."

"Your translator must be off. Put two fingers at the back of your neck."

I did it.

The things turned legible. I can read them.

"What happened? It happened to me one more time back when I escaped them earlier."

"Can you read them?"

"Yes."

"Okay, so put in H…EL…LIK…A…"

The projectors stopped, and the shield dilated into thin air.

He dashed out and started calling out 'Sara.'

"Who's Sara?" I asked.

"The lady from the apartment."

Yes, I know her name. I can't believe that I forgot her name.

"Yes, we'll look for her, but we have to free them out too."

"Who?"

"The people who saved us. Almost. The car?"

"Where are they?"

"There." I pointed him two cells away from his, and he ran to them.

"Hello bud," said Ryker.

"How did you know our coordinates?"

"You're welcome," scoffed Chloe.

"Tell me. Now! No one knows about this place except us. How did you guys breach in? It's about fifty feet down the ground in the middle of nowhere."

"Fifty feet down the ground?" shouted Carlos.

"Shut up," said Arleigh.

"You know what? I'm leaving this group. You, people, don't deserve me. I get no respect here. I told everyone going here is a stupid idea, and see where we are now. Just take me back. I'll be gone."

"Okay," everyone said simultaneously.

He scoffed and walked away.

"Tell me," sterned Arleigh.

"Why do we trust you," said Chloe.

"He's trustworthy. He'll do anything to keep me safe. He's been saving me from everything for so long."

Chloe sighed. He looked at Ryker. He nodded yes.

"The car. We found it from a crash site. It has the capability to jump through space and time. It creates a wormhole kind of thing. We used it to get here. It's top secret – the ship. Only we have its coordinates. All those weapons, the armors, the technology, everything. It was so advanced. Around a thousand years ahead of us. We believe it's from another world."

"What about our coordinates?"

"Can you unlock this shield? I would have to show it to you?"

Arleigh looked at me, and I nodded yes.

He swiped three fingers and put the password in. It dilated into nothing. She walked out and put her thumb between my eyebrows.

Arleigh's natural instinct was to push her away and break her hands, but I held his hand and signaled him 'no.'

She pressed and removed her thumb. A small ball thing came out fried and dropped to the floor.

"GPS. It has a three-dimensional output to the exact location. It's the same tech. Ryker and I knew it was beneath the surface."

"You gotta be kidding me!" Carlos shouted maniacally.

"Whatever," said Arleigh. "We need to find Sara. She knows what exactly is going on and maybe how to fight her."

"Who's Sara," asked Chloe. She didn't expect to find another person involved in this.

"I don't care who's she," said Ryker. "If she knows how to fight her, we gotta need her."

God, his voice is so deep.

Arleigh moved, and we followed him through. Carlos scoffed and started walking behind us.

Arleigh kept calling for Sara. I did too. We came across two divisions and parted ways into two groups. Arleigh called for him and me, and Ryker called for him and me.

"No, he's coming with me," said Arleigh.

"He's coming with me," said Ryker. "Neither Chloe nor I know the password to this cell shield. You both do. We can't read them, but you can. Take Chloe with you, and give him to me. He'll be safe."

"That makes sense," I said.

Arleigh conceded his thought after I assured him he was good and strong.

Chloe and I switched places.

"Take care of him," said Arleigh.

Ryker nodded, and we went in right.

It's been a while since we crossed paths. We still haven't seen her. I wonder how Crossa still hadn't found us. This quarter maybe was built differently. Separate from others. I looked around. There were no cameras, and the area, too, appeared intact. No damage from invasion.

"That day," said Ryker. "Why did you say it was not my fault?"

"What do you mean?"

"That day on the stairs. You were in a hurry to leave. You stared deep into my eyes. What did you see?"

His voice rose.

"You don't wanna know."

"I do!" His voice echoed throughout the quarter ways.

I knew if I told him the truth, it would break him. But did it really matter at this point in time?"

"Your wife," I said. "She died in a terrorist attack with your daughter, didn't they?"

Ryker stopped.

"You were the head general of the National Antiterrorism squad. You uncovered a group of possible Soviet assassins hired for the President. You were given all kinds of recognition and honored for your service."

"Make it stop," Ryker said. "How do you know?"

"That recognition took you to the red list of the Soviet attackers. They planned to take something much bigger than your life and leave you empty. Broken."

"No," he cried.

"One cold night while you were out of state serving around the borders. They broke into your house and shattered your life in this void of grief that you began hurting people. It left you broken just as they planned. At a bar, in an attempt to forget what happened, you met Chloe who invaded it to get in some bottles. That's where you found her to hide in your tears and started this group."

He broke and grabbed me by my neck against the wall. I coughed. The thrust was too strong.

"How do you know?"

"It's not your fault."

"HOW THE FUCK DO YOU KNOW?"

"When I looked into your eyes, I somehow saw your fears to your darkest secrets. This being the darkest of all," I said. "I'm sorry about everything."

Ryker dropped me to the ground. I coughed. That hurts. Ryker grabbed his head. I looked up at him. He pulled down a hand and pushed me up.

"Aaron?" It was Arleigh.

"I'm here," I shouted.

Ryker and I had a quick eye talk. It mostly meant to not tell anyone whatever happened here.

Arleigh came in running and approached me.

"Are you okay?"

"Yes," I said. "Why?"

"No, I heard screams."

"They must be the prisoners," I said. "They are filthy. They are not humans or animals. They look outrageous."

"They are the species from around the universe," said Ryker. "Aren't they?"

Arleigh looked at him with scrutiny.

I noticed and shook his arm.

"Why are you here, though?"

"I found something."

Chloe walked in with supporting someone. She had trouble walking. It was Sara!

She looked at me and fell to the ground. I ran to her. I took her hands, and she began crying. She caressed her hands on my face.

"I was worried about you," she said. "I am more than thankful that you're safe."

I felt a connection to her. I haven't felt this with anyone. It was pure. She hugged me tightly.

"I have the stone," I whispered in her ear.

"I know you do, sweetie."

"Dad's dead,"

"I know," she said. "Arleigh told me. He was not your real Dad."

"I know, Xalk is!"

Her jaw dropped.

"How do you know?"

"Dad told me."

"What more did he tell?"

Ryker coughed.

"We don't have time for this," said Ryker.

"Yeah, she'll be here anytime now," said Chloe.

"Who," asked Sara.

"Her name's Crossa, she's –"

"The queen of Eliospdkians," she said. "We need to get out of here. Quick!"

A huge metal whump was heard across the pathway. The creatures in the prison roared up. They all came close to the shield. They shrieked, and mixed alien chatters roared up the area.

"We need to find a way to get out of here," said Sara.

"The car. We need to get to it," said Arleigh.

"But how?" Asked Chloe.

"What's with the car," asked Sara.

"It can teleport through portals," Arleigh said.

Everyone nodded to Sara.

Ryker looked at me. "How did you get here kid?"

Everyone paused and locked eyes at me.

"How did you get here?" Asked Arleigh.

"I got transported here."

"Transported?" Arleigh thought for a while. His eyes rose. "Shit! Do you have the stone?"

I looked at Sara. She nodded. I nodded yes.

"Where's it?"

"In my bag."

I put the hand back in my bag. It was there. I pulled it out.

Everyone came closer to look at the stone in my fist.

"How does it work?" asked Arleigh.

"Dad told me to think about the place and feel that you are there. It will take you."

"Stop calling him Dad," warned Sara. "He told you the right thing."

Chloe looked at Ryker.

"It's vintage. You've sat in it, right? Try remember it."

"Hmm, okay."

"When have you sat in these goons' car," Said Sara. I need you to tell me whatever has happened to you till now!"

Chloe gasped. "I helped you up."

I nodded nervously.

"I will," I said. "Now everyone shut up."

I closed my eyes. The car. It's yellow. Leather brown seats. Ryker seating at driver's seat. Chloe messing with Ryker. Carlos being an ass. I am sitting on the window seat, peeking out through the window. Wind gushed through my hair as I put my hand on the handrest.

-

I opened my eyes. I had the stone in my hand. I was in the car. The window seat. Sara is beside me in the center. Arleigh is on the other side. Ryker was in the driving seat, and Chloe beside him in the front seat.

"It worked!" I screamed with joy.

Everyone laughed. The joy of us being saved. But too early. We have to get out. I looked out of the window. It was a well-lit room. Machinery was kept aside along with several large structures.

"We're in the laboratory," said Arleigh. "She could see us in the cam. We have to get out. Every bit of this area has a cam. This is their most fragile and robust quarter."

"Fuck!" Arleigh slammed the steering wheel quite a few times.

"What happened?" Asked Chloe.

"We don't have that sheet."

"God!" sighed Chloe

"What sheet?" Asked Arleigh.

"Well it has a code of various strange symbols and we found it in a sheet in that ship."

"Can you hotwire this? There has to be a way," said Arleigh.

"This has a different mechanism. I can't hotwire this," said Ryker.

"What's this tech," asked Sara.

"It's Xalkrea," smiled Arleigh. "It's true the ship's here on Earth."

She was baffled. She chuckled.

"It's with the goons," said Arleigh.

"Stop calling us that," Chloe turned and pointed to us with her finger. "We are very professional."

"Okay," Sara scoffed.

Chloe went insane on her.

"So is there any other way, Ryker?" Arleigh asked.

"Yeah, this either requires the code, which we don't have, or an authentication."

Arleigh's hopes rose. There was a power in his tone now.

"What kind of authentication?"

"A fingerprint, maybe."

"Fingerprint," said Arleigh.

Arleigh smiled. Sara smiled.

"It's his, isn't it," Chloe looked back and grinned after she noticed Arleigh smiling. "It's Aaron's fingerprint."

What? It's mine?

Ryker looked back.

"It's worth a try," there was a calmness in his voice now.

I moved forward and put on my thumb beside the steering. It scanned. Nothing happened.

"Nothing happened," said Arleigh.

"Give it a minute," said Sara.

Our sweat broke. The silence was deafening. We all had one thought - to get out of here. But that seemed to move away with every second that passed by. Coming this close to making our escape sounded vague now. What if our escape plan got terminated? What if Crossa comes in first? This is a nightmare.

The car revved up.

The systems came in. We cheered in a frenzy. This was the loudest cheer I have ever experienced after this wild tension.

I leaned back in the seat. I felt like a hero.

"Let's get out of here," said Ryker.

He pushed several keys in and swiped his fingers on the broken screen. The engines roared, and the car hovered up. It created a blue sphere shield around the car.

"I can't believe us six are going to get back," said Chloe.

"Six? We're five," I said.

"No," she said. "You, me, Ryker, Carlos, Arleigh, and Sara."

"Uhh, actually," I said. "We don't have Carlos."

"What?" She looked back and counted. "How is he not here?"

"He got lost. He was walking behind us when we split ways and I believe we lost him there. Also, we forgot about him. He's very forgettable I must say. Indeed, he could not get into the radius," said Arleigh.

"Who's Carlos," asked Sara.

"He was this very annoying guy, and he was always after me. He believes his friend died because of me and he finds ways to get back at me," I said. "You don't wanna know him."

"You didn't do anything," Sara said out of shock. "I didn't want him to die earlier. I have seen a lot of dead people in the last few days."

Sara scoffed.

"Whatever, we have to get him," Chloe said. "Perhaps get your issue sorted."

"No we don't," said Ryker. "He decided to leave the group. He's on his own now."

"Yeah," I said. "The issue is sorted. We left him."

"He was pissed. He doesn't mean it."

"Too bad," said Ryker.

"Why do you care," I said. "He was being too mean and he is a pain in the ass. You know that."

"I guess," she said. "He has the information about us. I'm afraid he'll give that to her."

"He's a coward," Ryker said. "He won't dare to go near her."

A shock wave detonated the area. The wall on either side was dusted into debris. The Eliospdkian walked in and thrusted himself up with her shoe jets, and reached near the car.

"Trogr," said Arleigh. "Hurry!"

"Just a second," said Ryker. "I am putting in the coordinates."

"You know him," said Sara.

"Arleigh!" He shouted.

"Yes, I do," Arleigh said. "He's thisrty for our blood and hungry for that stone."

He swung his sword at the shield, and it dissipated into dust. He was starstruck. His face turned white. His eyes said it all.

"Xalkrea," said Trogr. He gulped his saliva.

Chloe asked Sara to move. She didn't budge.

"Move away," Chloe said. "I have a plan."

I held Sara's hand and asked her to move in a hushed voice. She moved toward me, and I was squished to the opposite side. Chloe promptly punched in the middle of the back seat, and a gun blaster popped out. Arleigh smirked and held the gun. The slot went back in the seat. Chloe moved and nodded embarrassingly at Chloe.

"You should have said that it was the gun."

He slid the window down, charged the gun to full power, and shot it at him. He dodged the shots. Arleigh soon noticed the pattern in his movement and made the shot. It took him, and he crashed to the ground. Probably unconscious.

"He dead?" I asked.

"Yes, he is," Arleigh said. "But she isn't."

Crossa stood far along Trogr with fear in her eyes, as if she had not expected Xalkrean technology to still exist.

"Shoot her!" I shouted.

"This can't kill her," Sara said. "But that bought us time."

"Good shot, tiger," said Chloe.

Arleigh smiled.

"Got it," said Ryker. "We are ready to go."

A portal opened right before us.

Chloe looked at me.

I smiled.

Sara looked at me.

I smiled.

I looked at all of them.

"Just get me home."

THE PRESENT

TO BE CONTINUED…

About the Author

Krishang Agrawal

Krishang Agrawal is a young passion-driven seventeen-year-old marking his debut with 'The Escape Plan'. He lives in Khandwa, India, and loves anything related to space and science. He has contributed articles and podcasts to some Literary organizations and blogs which have given his writing various appreciations. Krishang is in his final year of school and will pass out next year in 2024. His passion is to pursue Aerospace Engineering alongside creative writing. His interest in science reflects in his works, which are mainly science-fiction and suspense-thriller. His works include several flash-fictions and short stories. This is his first novel, and he cannot be more thrilled to share his creative insights with the world.

www.ingramcontent.com/pod-product-compliance
Lightning Source LLC
LaVergne TN
LVHW041936070526
838199LV00051BA/2813